Texas Triangle Volume 1

by
Melvin Rea Katt

Order this book online at www.trafford.com
or email orders@trafford.com

Most Trafford titles are also available at major online book retailers.

Note for Librarians: A cataloguing record for this book is available from Library
and Archives Canada at www.collectionscanada.ca/amicus/index-e.html

Printed in Victoria, BC, Canada.

ISBN: 978-1-4269-0869-9 (sc)
ISBN: 978-1-4269-0870-5 (hc)
ISBN: 978-1-4269-0871-2 (eBook)

*Our mission is to efficiently provide the world's finest, most comprehensive book publishing
service, enabling every author to experience success. To find out how to publish your
book, your way, and have it available worldwide, visit us online at www.trafford.com*

Trafford rev. 9/14/2009

www.trafford.com

North America & international
toll-free: 1 888 232 4444 (USA & Canada)
phone: 250 383 6864 ♦ fax: 812 355 4082

ACKNOWLEDGEMENTS

I AM DEEPLY GRATEFUL to my deceased father for insisting that I experience city life rather than waste the rest of my days hanging around in the country. I could never say enough about my wonderful mother who is about ninety one years of age who has always shown great love to all of us and inculcated the pure essence of moral values.

I am most indebted to my friend Batiste who probably gave what I could not provide for myself. He took me under his wing like a father and kept me out of trouble. Special thanks to all of my friends and family in California who gave their support.

I wish to thank Numero Uno, (the head doctor) for adding a whole lot of fun to our lives.

I would like to thank my friend Ronnie Espinoza for assisting me in toying with the idea of designing a broken Texas equilateral triangle.

I greatly appreciate my children's contribution to this enormous endeavor. I would like to thank my oldest son, who is co-owner of Pendulum Architectural Studio for designing the book cover. Our hats go off to our youngest son for building the computers for this endeavor. And of course I am grateful to our wonderful daughter for giving me one of the computers to be rebuilt.

Most of all, my heart goes out to my lovely wife who is the most incredible person I've ever met. It has meant the world that she has always stood by me. She deserves nothing but the best.

INTRODUCTION

THE TEXAS TRIANGLE IS based on a true story. It is the exemplification of many small town struggles. The story is about a young man born and raised in Deadwood, Texas, thirty-four miles southwest of Shreveport, Louisiana and twenty-two miles northeast of Logansport, Louisiana. This book also explores the determination and strength of character possessed by a poor young black man.

The town consists of two general hardware stores surrounded by cotton fields and watermelon patches. It had no post office, mail was annexed from Logansport. To this day, Farm Road 31 (commonly known as Deadwood Road) is the front door and back door to and through the town. By the way, the town is not even on the map.

ABOUT THE AUTHOR

WHY PEOPLE WOULD WANT to Read This Book

It is truly intriguing. This story touches the hearts of people all across America and beyond. Readers are saying, "This book is like watching television in their own homes."

A NOTE FROM THE AUTHOR

ARCHITECTURALLY, A TRIANGLE OR pyramid is one of the strongest structures there is. In most situations it is difficult to brake free from within a triangle or a circle. I suppose I have worked different angles all of my life. I have lived in three states, Louisiana, Texas, and California. My wife and I have three children who are equally as strong and own at least three separate divisions of property and so do we.

I hope I haven't offended anyone by this books content. I spoke of Dad's children outside the marriage; however I want it to be known, they have shown nothing but respect for my Mom to this very day. After reading this book many of you realize the tactics used in the story are all too familiar. My message is this, "Keep on pushing when things are tough, later on they won't seem so rough".

All nick-names are real. In regard to the fellas, Doc named us all; however I assisted in nick-naming some of the girls.

All of the towns mentioned in this book are also real. Other names mentioned in the story are fictitious except for my friend Batiste, my oldest brother Ernie and his wife Gloria. To this day we still own land somewhere between the two native towns.

Three of my high school teachers, my barber, as well as a host of others gave me the nudge to push forward with this book.

I would like to thank all of my readers.

Melvin Rea Katt

CHAPTER ONE

IT WAS UNUSUALLY HOT and humid for an April morning. The midwife who we called Mama Flo, even though her real name was Floreece, was busying herself in the two bedroom shack in preparation for the birth of what everyone hoped would be a boy. Dad was particularly nervous as he sat on the front porch watching the kids run and jump about. With that rough, hoarse voice he called out, "Ain't dat rascal here yet, what it waitin' on?"

In reply Mama Flo who was very aggravated by this time said, "Kitt, you done done your job, now let me do mine, ya here?"

At that moment Dad got up and began pacing up and down the squeaky front porch. A few seconds later he heard the shrilling cry of a baby. Dad jumped straight up shaking the whole house. Mama Flo yelled out, "you betta stay out there, stay out there, ya here? Don't you come in here, at least give me a chance to clean the baby."

She wouldn't say if it was a boy or girl and Dad could hardly wait. He stopped dead in his tracks, waiting at the door. What took only a few minutes seemed to be hours. By now, he was so nervous with excitement, sweat began popping out all over his forehead.

Pushing open the door with the bundle in her arms, Mama Flo said, "Here he is, Kitty."

"Hee, hee, look at dis boy. He sho is pretty. He done broke da mold, look at him how he look at his daddy. I tell you, he sho got some pretty hair. I'm gonna name him uh, uh, M, uh, Mistah, yeah dats what I'm goin' name him Mistah." After weighting the baby on the cotton scales, Dad immediately turns still smiling then gives the baby to mama.

"Mama, ya know what I named dis boy? I just named him Mistah. Dis boy da one dat's gonna make us proud uf him. Yep, sho is."

Mom was a beautiful high yellow-skinned woman (a stone fox). She came from a racially mixed family. She proved to be kind and blameless in upholding the Golden Rule. Most relatives referred to her as Aunt Thelma.

When she worked, she cleaned and cared for the elderly white folks. To illustrate the mentality of the small country town, one of the old white men mom cared for said to her one day, "you sho got some big pretty legs." Besides that he wanted to feel them.

Being somewhat surprised, Mom said, "Mr. Tom, I thought you didn't like black folks."

Mr. Tom confessed, "I never said I didn't like the women, I don't like the men," was his reply.

Mom simply asked, "Why don't you feel Miss Annie's legs?"

His response was, "Oh, that's my daughter."

Mr. Tom had a cute little granddaughter. I liked her and she was crazy about me, Oh yeah, but them white folks didn't play that where we lived.

On the other hand dad was a hard nut to crack. His biggest regret was being poor and having to raise us in the rural of a small town.

Dad spent most of his pastime talking about how much he hated the white folks, at least most of them, dhem peckerwoods dis, dhem peckerwoods dat.

Mom would say, "Oh Kitt."

You see, he named himself Kitt, but his legal name was Thom Ira Katt.

Dad always wanted to be a big time cattle rancher, but never had the resources to fulfill his dream, nevertheless he kept trying. White folks would come by and tell him, "By god boy, if you gonna raise cows, git rid of the trees. If you gonna grow trees, by god, git rid of the cows".

2

Dad would just say, "Yah suh." As soon as they were gone, he yells out, "Kiss my black a--, you . . ." Since no one was there, we wondered who he was talking to. However, during their conversation neither of them had knowledge of Dad's five year old nephew sitting on the steps pointing his stuffed doll's middle finger straight at Mr. Charlie.

My Dad had five brothers and four sisters. In birth order the girls were, Aint Jenny, Aint Bip, Aint Sister and Aint Ruth. The boys were Uncle Booke, Uncle Mose, Uncle Bob, Uncle Melvin and Uncle Cecil.

He also had a whole bunch of first and second cousins and you could tell that they were truly related in one way or another.

Mom, Dad and baby sister

Dad was employed by the Carthage Independent School District, busing black kids fifteen miles each way to and from school across the Sabine River. He only stood 5' 6", sort of roly-poly at 250 pounds, with a slight bounce when he laughed. But that little man could really drive that bus. The bus he drove ironically was "Number 9", a hand-me-down, originally driven by the white folks, and after they finished farting it out (as my Dad said), then it was given to the blacks. The surprising thing about "Number 9" was that Dad could make that bus roll up a hill as fast as it would roll down the hill. All the kids raced to ride old juicy "Number 9" because it was so fast. During those days, the School Board felt that it was prudent to install a governor in each of the school buses to prevent the driver from speeding. Dad found a way to over-ride that little device. When he wanted to make up a little time after topping a hill he would really give it the gas and remove his foot off the accelerator, then the weight of the bus would increase the speed tremendously, passing up almost everything on the road. Oh, there were complaints, he simply reassured his boss, "Suh, you know yoself dees busses won't go dat fast. No suh." Case was closed.

The old man really had his own way of saying and doing things. When pulling up to a bus stop, he would swing open the front door and say, "you going, or you gonna git left. Well, git in den." He faithfully carried out this service for over fifteen years, and then he was fired just like that. The explanation given was that the school board was cutting back. He had worked the longest. What a shock? The first black man hired, and the very first man to be fired.

After being unemployed for more than a year and a half, Dad finally landed a job with the International Paper Company working in the forest. Even though the white folks helped him to get the job he still didn't trust them, not one little bit. Everyday my old man would pack a loaded 38 Special in his lunch pail, and when he went into the woods to work he would transfer it to his overalls pocket. I was told more than once, "I ain't gonna let dhem peckerwoods kill me and da make like it wus uh accident, if da do, I'll tell you one thang, I'll take a lot uh dhem so-and-so's wit me."

Dad in overalls

I have to admit regretfully that Dad was a real stinker. He had a weakness for those high-yellow women. We didn't know this about the ol' man until we got into junior high school. There were other kids walking around school calling my Dad 'Daddy'. In fact, they would go to the bus and say hi to him after school had been out for the day. Mom knew but she never breathed a word. It was at school where we got the real low down on the fella. When my next oldest brother, who everyone called Lil Kitt and I figured it all out we both cried.

The teachers would not consent to calling me Mister, but always referred to my full legal name, feeling that calling me Mister would somehow give me a psychological advantage or make me mannish.

Ms. Willie told me emphatically, "I don't care what your folks call you at home, your name is Melvin Rea Katt, and that is what you are going to be called around here, you hear me?"

"Yes Ma'am," was my reply.

I began to develop a strong personality, not by design, but perhaps due to growing pains. I always had a fondness for expressions, not only verbally but instrumentally as well, so I took up public speaking, and played a brass instrument in Turner High Bobcat band and grabbed mom's acoustic guitar every chance I got. I was assigned my own personal speech instructor, who everyone affectionately called Aint Dute. She was real neat and she liked my style.

She would confidently say, "baby, look at the audience, work the floor, work the judges, make them feel what you feel, and you keep that up and no one will ever be any better than you."

Oh, man! That was fun.

It was when I became a senior at Turner High School, I thought all my disappointments with Dad had finally come to an end, and along came something else that would start it all over again. Occasionally, I could hardly wait for the lunch bell to ring to make a mad dash for the band room where I grabbed my horn and closed the practice room door behind me. I had that

Coronet squealing creative notes way above the staff, somewhere in treble-clef.

The band director would come and knock on the door and say, "Hey, Melvin Rea, someone must have really made you mad." He then walked away.

Dad as always failed to make things any better. He told one of my half-brothers not to mess with them gals down the lane because they just might be his sister. I felt that he never showed our Mother the essence of true love. He never sat down with us and had a family discussion, or even talk with us individually in a kind manner, he would rather tip upon us and administer harsh discipline wherever he found us.

I never will forget when I was outside behind the little house taking a leak, he came out of nowhere and said, "Hey Mistah, when you finish school you ain't gonna stay round here cuttin' pulpwood and fixin' fences fur dees white folks. You goin' to California to stay wit yo Lil Aunt, so you kin make something out uf yoself. I don't want you comin' up like I did, plowin' mule's fur fifty-cent uh day. You know yoself, smelling dhem mule's funky butts is worth mo den fifty-cent. Go out yonder, git you a job making big money so you can help me and yo mama, cause we sho ain't gittin' no younger, you know. Dees other young sorry ni---- stay 'round here sayin', 'ya suh, no suh,' kissin' dees white folks butts, if you thank you gonna do dat, dats yo booty-wooty. If you do it you show ain't gonna do it 'round here, least in California you'll git 'nough money fur it. Like I done told you, some uf dees young sorry black a-- ni---- don't wont to work at-tall. Da thank da puddy, (pretty) but da ain't half as puddy as I is. When you git out yonder, don't you be nobody's fool, don't give dhem old women yo money, just laugh and talk and shoot the breeze wit um, then go on 'bout yo business, cause dhem old wo-out women sho don't mean you no good. Marry you a young woman so ya'll kin have somethin', no matter how much you read the Good Book boy, it ain't gonna keep yo pecker from gittin' hard."

He then peeps around the front of me and says, "yep, you sho gonna have a big'un, hee, hee," and disappeared.

The nerves of dad talking like that. I could in no way condone his immorality. Although, I didn't agree with his life choices, I respected him for wanting the very best for his children.

The big day finally arrived when Mister Katt received his diploma. Dad being more determined than ever for me to go to California, the night of graduation instructions was handed down.

"Git all yo stuff together, cause day after tomorra you gonna leave here boy, fur California. You gonna catch de first thang smokin' and don't tell me dat you got to go by to see dis gal and dat gal, cause you gonna git on dat Trail Way bus and go out yonder so you kin start a future fur yoself."

I pleaded with Dad, "just let me go see Super Fox before I leave." His reasoning was profound.

"Oh no, no - - - hell no, you might not come back and catch dat bus." Dad just wasn't having it. He was afraid of me not catching the bus as a billy goat is of a butcher's knife.

Bus and Train Depot
Picture from Panola County Museum

Sure enough two days later, right after day-break the family and I arrived before time to catch the bus at the train and bus station in Carthage. Carthage was so small you could stand on top of the courthouse and wee-wee all over town. I remember so well that we were all hugging and kissing good-bye as I was holding on to that twenty dollar bill dad had given me for spending change.

"You gonna catch this bus boy?" asked the driver.

"Yes, sir."

"You better git on in here then, I don't have all day to wait on you and put that guitar up top." As the bus drove off I could see that everyone was sobbing, I knew that all of them would miss me, but I had to go and make a man of myself. Someday they would be proud of me. While riding out on the 1960 Golden Eagle I had plenty of time to think about my career, after all, I had already gone to several country barber shops in Texas, even those guys were doing alright at a dollar a head.

After traveling for two days the driver yelled, "Los Angeles Bus Terminal, all depart from the rear door." As I looked around while collecting my old taped up luggage I was truly amazed at the size of the terminal and all the foot traffic going one place or the other. There were black folks and white folks of all shapes and sizes. It was incredible; I had never seen so many people in one place at one time in my whole life. Nevertheless, I was glad to be in the big city. Looking back now, I am sure I looked like a lost child, needing to be rescued from the crowd, but who steps up, none other than Lil Aunt and my cousin Dottie. We all hugged and exchanged kisses, we were very happy to see each other. At a glance, anyone could tell we were related.

I always thought that speaking was what I did best; therefore, I began to lay it on the ol' girls.

"This is really something, being escorted not by one, but two women, you know I deserve that, because I am Mister Katt, and don't you forget that."

Lil Aunt seemed to be somewhat shocked and looked at me with displeasure, but did not make a reply. Dottie shrugged her shoulders wondering what I would say next, but of course, she didn't think it was funny either.

They took me to their house in Watts otherwise known as South Central L.A., and showed me my new home. It was nothing but a little room out back that looked something like a chicken coop, added on to the back of the house with two bunk beds. There was no carpet or rugs, just a cold concrete slab floor. I was told that it was once a patio without a roof.

It had only one window facing the alley; my scenic view was the garbage cans. If I wanted to see anything interesting at all, I had to come from the back of the house down the driveway to the street.

Lil Aunt was one of my mother's older sisters and looked a little like her. At the age of fifty she was still a very attractive woman, soft spoken, but qualified to raise much hell.

Dottie, who was about thirty, was sharp as a tack, cute, but a bit skinny.

"How do you like your new room?" she asked.

"This is alright, but I thought I was going to get your room".

"Did you really? That room out there is good enough for you buster."

Lil Aunt didn't want me standing on the front lawn because the girls riding by would holler out their cars, "Hey baby."

I heard her tell Dottie, "You know that boy is sure stuck on himself, and he thinks he is so good looking."

"Oh, yes" says Dottie, "He loves the skin he's in."

"But I have news for him; we'll see how he's going to look when I tell him all the work that he has to do around here."

CHAPTER TWO

BEFORE I GO ANY further, allow me to dispense with my family's idiosyncrasies, and take a few minutes to tell you a little about the town in which I lived. First of all I sincerely believe that California is a black man's paradise, at least for the most part. Practically all southerners who moved west, ended up in Watts (South Central Los Angeles) or Compton, California, and many of them either married or got them a white woman. Watts was unique. There was 103rd Street, the heart of Watts, Jordon Downs, low riders, and cruisers from the soul side of town. It had just about anything the community wanted - theaters, clothing stores, pawn shops, appliance stores, Pop's Soul Burgers, and a few factories here and there. Not far away was an ABC Market which catered to the kind of food southern people liked to cook. A few blacks were employed by the City and County which had sub offices in and around the area, and of course, the famous Watts Towers was nearby.

Dottie was a strong advocate for history and wanted to expose me to as many cultural events that were available. For example, she took me to see the Watts Towers. Gazing up at the structures she tells me that the Watts Towers were constructed single handedly by a self-taught immigrant by the name of Simon Rodilla. In his spare time it took over thirty-three years to complete the project. He built the towers with no special equipment or design. I even climbed the thing. I could readily see much of its contents. There was lots of steel, rocks, and cement. I noticed other objects such as broken china, pieces of glass, seashells and soda pop caps that neighborhood children brought to him in hopes that he would add them to the project. Dottie told me that most of his material was damaged pieces of pottery from where he worked. She wanted me to know that this was once considered an eye-sore and threatened demolition. I go, "yeah, I can see why". I was impressed when she said these towers are now recognized as a significant work of art and a national landmark. Perhaps I could become famous someday.

The police station, known as the 77th Precinct was conveniently located to ensure peace. Public transportation wasn't too, too terrible, we had the red bus (Watts bus) that took passengers across town to the Metropolitan Connection (green bus) from there, passengers could go anywhere in Los Angeles, as well as out of town by getting off down town at L.A. Bus Terminal. The scary part was being sure that Metro didn't cause anyone to miss that Watts connection before sundown, if so, you better call somebody, because shortly after dark the red bus would no longer run.

As more and more blacks migrated to the city, many whites moved from the cities to the suburbs. The cities became increasingly populated with more blacks. In other words, the blacks had the city; the whites, the suburbs. When the blacks moved into a subdivision, the whites would move to another one, more expensive and farther away. In the middle 1960's the median annual income for black families was about $5,000; while that of the white families was about $9,300. The unemployment rate for blacks was over twice that for whites. In time what was once very nice areas had now become slums (ghettoes). Despite changing conditions many blacks and several whites who remained in areas within the area became known as ghetto-fabulous, which meant that they had nice cars, nice clothes, gold jewelry and well manicured lawns, things like that.

At present, in the 21st Century, the Watts district of South Central Los Angeles has changed the names of a lot of the streets. Watts' neighborhoods are bounded by 108th Street, Central Boulevard and 107th Street on the north; Wilmington and Croesus Avenue, which I lived about half way the block on the east, Imperial Highway was on the south, Compton Avenue and Central Avenue on the west. It is now served by 103rd Street/ Kenneth Hahn Station on the Blue Line and the Imperial/ Wilmington/Rosa Parks Street on the Blue and Green Lines of the Los Angeles Metro System.

One thing I learned early, the way Californians dressed was so different from that of East Texans. Plaid and floral shirts wasn't going to work in California. One other thing, Texas style of shoes just didn't measure up. The dressy apparel for young men at the time was the era of the Hoodlum Priest wardrobe. All the hipsters wore iridescent colored suits, no cuff in the slacks, coats buttoned straight up the front without any lapels, but fully styled with a permanent priest collar. The Hoodlum Priest was designed with a cloth band across the back waist of the coat, and a belt hanging down each rear side, accompanied by a pair of Italian boots which gave the appearance of a cool lightweight gangster. With that style of dress and slight hop in a young man's walk, it was on. It was real hip-like.

With what I had seen so far, alternatively I needed to make a 360 degree turnaround. In the imagination of my mind, I'm thinking to myself that I need a quick fix for poverty. Living with women telling me what to do, what to say, how to act, what I needed was independence. After all, before leaving East Texas, I told everyone, "when I come back I will be driving a car so long, it will take me a week to turn the corner and a week and a half to park it."

The new revelation was about to unfold. I thought it was only fair to advise the ol' girls of my decision. Without hesitation I told Lil Aunt and Dottie, "first thing tomorrow morning I'm going out to find me a job, so I can improve my lot in life."

"That's what you are going to need" says Lil Aunt, "I know one thing, those little pissy tail girls will get you in a lot of trouble. I heard them out there hollering at you, and you grinning like a chess cat. You better let those little girls go about their business.

Me and Dottie can't be taking care of any babies, and I sure ain't."

Sure enough, bright and early the next day I was off to a vigorous search for a job. I paraded up and down Alameda Street to a number of factories, from there to 103rd Street seeking to land a job in one of the stores. All day long I walked. I was not even permitted to fill out not one application. After such an exhausting search for employment practically wearing out the soles on the shoes I wore from Texas, I returned home to Lil Aunt's house.

"Well Mister! What time do you start work tomorrow?" asked Lil Aunt.

"I didn't find a job today, but tomorrow I am going downtown and I am sure that some of the businesses need a good looking young man like me."

"What did they say to you where you went?"

"Well, all of them wanted to know if I had any experience, so you know the answer to that. You just wait until tomorrow; I know I will come back with something,"

"Okay, well we will see," said Lil Aunt.

As confident as I was the next day's search ended with the same disappointment. It was indeed depressing and difficult trying not to show it as I tried to creep back in the house unnoticed. Who met me at the door, none other than cousin Dottie. Before she could ask, "The answer is no", was my reply.

"Well, hot stuff, I could have told you that. People out here must have a trade. They have to go to school and specialize in something in order to get a job. A little country boy like you can't come to the big city and take a job. There are grown men who are not employed. If you really want to be something, you'll have to enroll in school."

"Well, I will go to school then".

"Even with that under consideration, I'm not thoroughly convinced that you will be accepted. For one thing Texas curriculum is not quite up to snuff. You will probably have to take an entrance exam. And some country people are so slow. They talk slow, they walk slow, they are just slow period."

"Dottie, you just crossed the line. I can talk twice as fast as you and think seven times as fast as you."

"Yeah, but you don't be saying nothing. Okay Mister, what do you want to be?"

"I really would like to work with electronics, or be a barber."

"Now to be an electronic technician, um- that would require a minimum of two to four years of schooling, which means a whole lot of studying."

"No, no, that's too long; I need something that I can finish real quick. How long does it take to become a barber?"

"Oh, it takes about six months, and then you will have to take the State Board of Barber Examination."

Of course, that was her educated guess. Before Dottie and I could finish our conversation, Lil Aunt dashes in from the kitchen, puts her hands on her hips and goes into her hell-raising act, "I tell you one thing pretty boy, between now and September, you are gonna have to do some work around here. You are gonna have to earn your keep. This house need painting, the lawn need cutting, there's plenty of mopping and dusting to be done around here too. And every day I want these beds made up, and when I come in, there better not be even one dirty dish sitting around."

This did not sit too well with me, women telling me what to do, but I went along with the program in order to get what I needed. I tell you my determination was something to be admired despite the old goats' criticism, realizing I was limited to a certain degree. The things that kept me going was my inward desire to be successful, having unlimited resources and having neat friends around, both male and female, especially female. Of course my dad's words kept ringing in my ear, "go out yonder and make something uf yoself and keep yo head on straight." I suppose these words were the most exhilarating ones. It was also rejuvenating to remember the old man's humorous expressions such as, "Pussy ain't nothin' butta cat."

The funniest thing about that was when my brother told the old man, "We ain't got no cat."

I must say, these things kept me on my feet when my face was against the wind. Due to circumstances, laughter was good for me. Dad was always a cause for laughter, his singing was downright ridiculous, but comical, nonetheless. His favorite song was 'The Old Gray Mare'. As he bounced through the house and out the back door with his shotgun on his left shoulder his song went like this: "The old gray mare was floating down the Delaware, raising up her underwear, showing what was under there. Yep, the old gray mare just ain't what she used to be."

Back in the day, older folks never failed to amaze me, especially when it came to disciplining other people's kids and persons younger than themselves. One day Dad was working deep in the bottoms and decided, since he was tired it was best to come in at noon and rest. There was one older lady who came up to visit and couldn't get the gate open. Dad heard her, but never got up to assist her, and when she finally got in the house, she slapped him. After she left he told Mom emphatically, "If dat old lady hadn't been old I woulda whipped dat old ladies behind, slapping me." Every time I think about stuff like that I get tickled.

One thing about my Mom's side of the family, embarrassing any of them in any form or fashion was a no, no. Dottie took me shopping on the other side of town in Huntington Park, where she purchased me a very nice navy blue suit with all accessories to match and a black pair of Italian boots. The suit was on the hoodlum priest style, but with a twitch of conservativeness. Of course, this suit, unlike the hoodlum priest, was designed with a collar and lapels. With the brand new suit and fancy necktie, I was a knockout, and that's no lie. There was also a cloth band permanently attached to the back of the suit to give it a little pizzazz. I was convinced, my new attire was dazzling. In fact, sometimes I couldn't stand myself.

September had come and cousin Dottie was on the ball. She had already made arrangements for me to take my training at one of the barber colleges, on 5th and San Julian Street, right in the heart of skid-row in downtown Los Angeles. The school was for beginners, and appropriately so. The school used wine-os as guinea-pigs. All services were free, haircuts, shaves, shampoos and really, their whole body needed shampooing. This was quite a task, because all the wine-os and old men from the missions on 5th Street had long, dirty hair and beards. They were very fowl smelling, down-right funky. If not skid-row, where else would a beginner get a client? The only thing that separated the filth and funk from decent people was several sets of railroad tracks running parallel to Alameda Street downtown.

Every morning Dottie would drop me off at 5th and Main, in her old beat-up 1950 Buick Special. I would jump out of the old car with my tool kit in one hand and my lunch in the other hand, and trot off to San Julian Street.

The first order of the day, shortly after roll-call was to go next door to the classroom where the instructor lectured on theory for about thirty minutes. The back section of the college was designated for learning how to give a shave. Our very first client was a hard plastic mannequin. The procedure was done as if I had a real live person, starting with the chair cloth, washing the hands and draping the mannequin. The next step was to tilt the chair back, lather the face and steam it with a hot towel; sterilize the razor and follow all the steps of shaving.

Noteworthy, the shave was done with a dummy razor (not a real razor blade, it couldn't cut butter) therefore the student could not lacerate the mannequin or cause injury to himself. After practicing shaving the mannequin for three or four days I was ready for a real live turkey (person), using real tools from the barber kit. Oh, I tell you those wine-o's beards were just about as tuff as nails and plenty dirty. I had to lather it up at least three times and apply a steaming hot towel many times to soften the beard.

To beat all, some of the wine-os would fall asleep while in my chair and besides that, some of them would have food in their mouth. That would really gross you out. Some days it seemed like everyone that came in had lice in their hair and beard. We declared those days as national lice day. I was so happy when that day ended. Nevertheless, I come to realize that those things came with the territory. However, don't let their appearance fool you. They weren't always bums. Their street name is Wino, but the technical name is The Homeless. Somewhere, life made a dreadful twist.

Many of them were once husbands, wives, fathers and mothers. In that quaint category a number of them are resourcefully efficient. At one time or another they were classified among many as; social worker, secretaries, lab tech's, electricians, plumbers and many other titles in our thriving industry. Amazingly, some of those guys on skid-row could tap into Water & Power as well as Edison Electric resources with the greatest of ease. The better dressed ones seem to be paranoid. Even-though I trained on skid-row my instructor was fanatic about punctuality.

This particular morning I felt that I was running late, so I approached a black guy on the street who was wearing a khaki suit and army cap, "Hey Sir, could you tell me what time it is?

Then I noticed him looking a little weird, he said, "Nah, nah, I know what you're up to, you git on away from me!" He crossed the street in a frantic rage.

Something drastic must have happened to those guys for them to be out on the streets. Among the wine-os on the streets of Los Angeles are professional beggars who dress up like bums. A good beggar on the streets rakes in about thirty thousand dollars a year, tax free, and the beat goes on. And it's really amazing how they work holidays and weekends, beggars don't take breaks, and besides that they use bus passes to go wherever people are.

There were only a few black patrons on skid-row. The wine-o demography was primarily of the Caucasian race. The school was like a revolving door. It remained open year round. As the students advanced they were transferred to a much better environment located on Main Street. Advanced students were replaced by new ones checking in on skid-row. Needless to say, my skills had vastly improved and I thought it was prudent to learn how to cut straight hair.

After being there for two months the instructor says to me, "Kattman, Monday you will be going over to Main Street. Check in with Mr. Lucky at eight o'clock Monday morning".

"Thank you; it's been a pleasure having you as an instructor."

"Thank you, you will do real well up there."

Monday morning I checked in with Mr. Lucky. He says to me "Mister Katt, I saved you a nice chair, it's near the front. Chair number "9", you think you will like that?"

"Oh yes, I like that."

"Go set up your station and I will send you someone as soon as possible."

I was also greeted by a couple of friends who left skid-row two weeks before me. It was so refreshing to be on Main Street. Now I can stop holding my breath. That was exactly what I said, after leaving such deplorable conditions.

The guys on skid-row had not combed their hair since I don't know when, hadn't brushed their teeth or washed their face and who knows what else.

Now Main Street was an entirely different clientele; practically no more crew cuts or flat tops. Up here, there were more business-like styles and the progressive look. Hair cuts were seventy-five cents and fifty-cents for a shave. By the way, the funds went to the school, except when the instructors weren't around.

Theory was taught twice a day. Half of the class went for instruction at eight o'clock in the morning for one hour, while the rest of them attended at one o'clock in the afternoon. School at this stage of my training was really interesting. Since the scope of barbering is the head, face and neck, I was flabbergasted to know that I must learn the circulatory vascular system and how it relates to barbering. We all had the assignment of tracing the blood from the heart to the lungs and back to the heart. I had previously studied biology in high school, but we didn't really have good books. When my school was notified that the blacks would be getting new books, some of my books had someone else's name in them.

The theory of barbering changed my whole attitude about learning. An in-depth look at the circulatory system revealed much about design and order. The heart is described as the pump of the body. The interior of the heart contains four chambers and valves. The upper chambers are the right atrium and left atrium. The lower chambers are the right ventricle and the left ventricle. They are the real work horses; for they must force the blood away from the heart with sufficient power to push the blood all the way back to the heart. In the average person, the heart beats about seventy two times a minute.

More study was required in order to become efficient in this area of learning. The heart is responsible for pumping the blood to every cell in the body. It is also responsible for pumping blood to the lungs, where the body gives off carbon dioxide and takes on oxygen. The heart is able to pump blood to areas efficiently because there are dual circulatory circuits with the heart as the common link.

In the pulmonary circuit, the blood leaves the heart through the pulmonary arteries, goes to the lungs, and returns to the heart through the pulmonary veins. The blood leaves the heart through the aorta; then goes to all the organs of the body. We were taught that arteries always carry blood away from the heart, and veins carry blood toward the heart. Most of the time, arteries carry oxygenated blood and veins carry deoxygenated blood.

We were taught a lot of memory aides, for example, when trying to remember the blood flow, just say, 'when the blood leaves the right side, it comes right back, nevertheless, when it leaves the left side, it is still left.' This study gave me a better sense of the possible complications of the heart. With all honesty, I thought maybe I could help relatives to appreciate taking care of such a valuable organ. I came to realize that the heart is chief in its functions. The blood it pumps helps to equalize the body temperature and also protects the body from extreme heat and cold. It assists in protecting the body from harmful bacteria and infections, by means of the white blood cells, and it's helpful in many other ways too.

I was definitely intrigued with the medical terminology on infectious diseases. Terms common to the trade, such as:

Tinea Barbae: ring worm of the beard
Tinea capitis: ring worm of the scalp
Tinea Faciei: ring worm of the face
Tinea corporis: fungus affecting the skin and the body
Tinea manus: ring worm of the hands
Tinea pedis: athlete's foot
Tinea crusis: itch of the groin
Tinea nodosa: ring worm of the mustache

Other terms were:

Trichonosis: any disease of the hair
Trichonocardiosis: ring worm of the skin and scalp

At this point, I began to feel like I was riding high, learning terms used by physicians. I know you are saying that I am doing quite well right about now. I was, but not at home. Putting up with Lil Aunt and Dottie for several months was a grueling test of my humility, strength and courage. Oh, they both knew that I attended school five days a week and half day on Saturday, yet at any time Lil Aunt just had to go into one of her hell raising acts.

"You are just too lazy for me; you sleep too much for a man, don't half clean up, you play that radio too loud and then on top of that, you think you're pretty, the only ones pretty around here are me and Dottie, because we take care of your pissy tail, and I tell you one other thing, you better not flunk that barber's exam. When your six months are up you are on your own buddy. Your brother Junior is going to be here about the first week of June and you will have to help him just like me and Dottie helped you. That's why I spent my money on that room and bunk beds."

By the way, Junior was the name close relatives called Lil Kitt.

The ol' girls knew they had me over a barrel, and I was hipped to the fact that if I didn't hit that cold cement floor early every morning, and stayed in that bunk bed, Dottie would automatically leave me. She knew I was an enthusiastic student of the trade for she would listen very attentively to me studying medical terminology on diseases. After ease dropping on me studying, Dottie now knew without a doubt that any of those types of streptococcus and pathogenic diseases could be transmitted from one person to another. She told me, "don't you be bringing them trichonocardiosis in here to me and Lil Aunt, you leave that smock you wear at school until the weekend, then put it in a bag and you bring it home and throw it in the washing machine, wash it and then you can take it back." Consequently I had to do so.

I had to learn to be a good student which required much more than purchasing a new text book. Owning a Los Angeles Library card was a step in the right direction. A text book will no doubt keep a person within the scope of their trade, but library books will really take you far beyond. Dottie accused me of not using a great deal of variety in my reading and research. I concluded that if I really wanted a person to know something that I didn't want to tell them personally, just simply leave the evidence in their path, slightly obscured to the human eye and a nosey person will surely find it. Here's what I did, I decided to drop my library card on the floor slightly under the kitchen table. Guess what? It worked.

When I had the time to meditate on their methods, I figured out that ridiculing me emanated from their crazy idea that this type of conduct would make me a better man.

But I really feel that Main Street prepared me for the real world. There were so many different personalities, people wanting something different. I learned what to say and how to greet different types of people. Homosexuals black and white paraded the school floors looking for services we weren't trained for. Consequently the instructors ran them out of the college.

Students who were close to completing their schooling were permitted to practice on each other in preparation for state board. As the instructor stood closely monitoring the students, my most embarrassing moment occurred when one of my fellow class mates asked if I would mind giving a scientific rest facial; of course I didn't mind. The facial required messaging the forehead, ears, and eyes, around the nose, lips, cheeks, and back of the neck. Just as I began the ninth movement, Mr. Lucky yelled from the back of the school "Hey Katt, ------ cut HER loose!" The entire school of forty-eight students burst out in laughter. Mr. Lucy's little caper was most embarrassing for me and the girl.

I was becoming a good student of life, but nonetheless I was just a little naïve to the real meaning of bigotry. 92nd street crossed Alameda and the railroad tracts into Southgate which separated South Central from the so called better class. On occasion I walked across the tracts to Southgate for no particular reason. Surprisingly on the way back Caucasians coming through South Central to Southgate yelled out of their car, "Get back cross the tracts." I couldn't imagine what they were saying. It took me three minutes to figure out they were telling me I didn't belong on that side of the tracks. On another occasion I wasn't anywhere near crossing the tracks, a family in a pickup truck passed me by while the little boy standing in the seat began shooting at me with his toy pistol, thanks to the boy's mother, she pushed his hand down. The kid had just filled the Katt full of lead. The good thing about this is I survived.

Thank goodness, the time had arrived that I had been waiting for--to take the state examination for my barber license. I applied in April and received a date to take the test the same month. I felt real good about the exam, I thought I had found my niche. I was okay with medical terminology, excellent with laws, rules and regulations. Most of all I was a master on the floor. Right before the exam I went out and bought myself a brand new smock, with a "v" neckline and lapels so it would show off my necktie, perhaps that might empress the judges, I thought. To this day I still don't know how I found the money to buy that new smock.

The exam was scheduled to be held at my school. Thirteen chairs were partitioned off upstairs. Each participant was given a number and must be in the waiting room with his or her live model when their number was called by one of the three examiners.

One hour was allotted for the exam, each minute over time; one point was deducted from the participant's score. A haircut, shave, rolling cream massage, a scientific rest facial and a neckline had to be given, all in one hour. The written and oral examination was given down stairs after finishing the practical part of the exam. The examiners used the numbers from one to forty-nine that day, when the examiner called number "9" I answered, "here".

He said, "You have five minutes to seat your patron and setup, wait for the okay to start your examination."

With eager anticipation, I hurried to my chair, seated my patron, and stood waiting for the signal to begin. The starting signal was given as the examiners continued to call participant's numbers. The variance of sound in each person's pair of clippers could be heard as they hummed its own tune. With the rap of the combs and the clicking of the shears, it produced the sound of music.

At an instant the sounds seemed to soften to a whisper when the Kattman did a two minute creative solo with the rhythmic strapping of my newly purchased razor. One of the examiners, a fussy looking little man with an English mustache came down from his elevated booth and walked over to my chair. Oh man, that shook everyone up except me. Guys were so concerned with me and the examiner they were missing movements and stuff. In their minds they thought the examiner was coming to chastise me. It caught them off guard. The examiner commences to telling me, "Young man, we need more men like you in the field."

"Thank you sir."

I go home just rolling with excitement and a sense of accomplishment. I entered the house, "Lil Aunt, Lil Aunt."

"What you want boy?"

"I just know I passed the barber's exam".

"Good for you because your rent starts today buddy boy. You will have to buy your own food, clothes and anything else you need, because today you are on your own."

My excitement vanished instantly. I was confused.

"Lil Aunt", how can my rent start today when I don't even have a job? I just took the board today; it will take approximately two weeks before I know whether or not I passed, I don't even have a place to work yet."

"Well you better get your heels to clicking then."

I stood petrified, but I knew the ol' girl meant business. Needless to say, an honest search for a shop to work in was underway. By the way, a friend told me about a community barber shop that might need a barber. Without hesitation I went over to meet the owner. To my surprise the owner was a lady, her name was Jean. She welcomed me to the field and assured me a chair in her shop as soon as I received my license.

I was relieved just a little because I knew this was only the second step. I had two weeks to wait for the state board's reply. Going back home wasn't any fun at all. As I waited for the results I wasn't nervous about it, for I thought I pretty much had it in the bag. Exactly two weeks later I received a letter stating, *"Congratulations, you have successfully passed the State of California Barber's Examination."*

That Saturday, I immediately called Jean and gave her the good news. She told me to come in Tuesday because the shop was closed on Mondays. I began to set my mind on a prosperous new future in the field of barbering.

CHAPTER THREE

Round One

IT IS TUESDAY, DAY one. Jean was pleased to have me and immediately assigned me the first of the four chairs she had in her shop. I was told that this was once an all women's shop and they had more business than they could handle. Men folk just loved having women rubbing on them, and especially if they were as fine as the Jeanettes. The women looked good and they also smelled good and the male customers came dressed-to-kill. Once a ruckus broke out, simply because one client felt the lady barber was giving another client more attention than he was getting.

Over the course of time for one reason or another, women usually have to stop work. Jean decided to try her hand with men barbers; in my case, a young man. It was customary for the rookie barber to have the front chair, so when clients came in, he would have first shot at them. The first day was a getting acquainted day; not much business. I arrived back home about nine o'clock in the evening. The first thing out of the ol' girl's mouth was the big question.

"How many heads did you cut today?"

I was quite reluctant to answer, but responded by saying, "three or four."

"Three or four?" Dottie asked. "At two dollars a head how are you going to pay rent cutting only three of four heads a day? You are already two weeks behind. You got to do better than that sweetie."

They casually walked through the house saying to each other "three or four heads," then busted into laughter.

This was a bit humiliating making light of my humble beginning, but not to the point of blowing my cool. Sometimes I wondered if they really wanted me to succeed. I finished the week okay. The word soon got around that Jean got a new barber in her shop, and cute at that.

"Girl, what's his name? Girl, I don't know, I just know he is fine."

From that day forward foot traffic began to increase. Girls and women of all kinds continued to walk past the shop, peeking in as they walked by. Three to five minutes later the cycle was repeated. Being a new barber and a young man, I had no idea what was going on. Jean advised me that the women were checking me out.

As the weeks progressed, some of them actually came in and requested services from Jean. I suppose this was a way to get a closer look. Sometimes I thought my presence was creating more business for Jean than myself. Meanwhile, getting to work proved to be quite a challenge, walking from 92nd and Croesus, to 92nd and Compton Avenue to catch the Watts bus to 58th and Compton, and then footing it eight blocks to the barber shop. It literally took me an hour and a half to reach my destination. Now I began to wonder would I make enough money in this business to sustain myself.

Here is what we have: a community barber shop verses a business district barber shop. A business barber shop is somewhat like the man betting on the dice, he might not see the same head twice. The community barber shop requires an honest effort to build the business and hope for return customers. Of course this was definitely Jean's recommendation. Like my old man always said, *quitters never win and winners never quit.* Therefore, I decided to take on the challenge of being a business builder rather than being a splitter or a quitter.

It was obvious that I did fabulous work; nevertheless, all the guys wanted Jean. After watching my masterpieces on first timers, some of Jean's clients would allow me to cut their children's hair.

Sometimes Jean had her clients waiting so long for her to come in, they had no other choice but to let me cut their hair or come back another day. Oh, I failed to mention that we did have an older man in the barber shop, but he couldn't cut his way out of a paper bag. There was something truly amazing about the barber shop. Every big lie ever told, was conceived and given birth to in the barber shop. It's sort of like every baby being born on February 29th only has a birthday every three years. One of my customers told Jean, "I can cook, I can burn, I am a chef. If you don't believe me ask Tony." He goes on to say, "I work for Norm's on Sunset in Hollywood. Jean, I was the head Chef at the Lord's Evening Meal." I have to admit that was quiet amusing.

By mere coincidence, something great happened. One Sunday afternoon I did not want to sit around looking Lil Aunt and Dottie in the face, so I walked down to 103rd Street to see a movie. To my surprise I saw two guys who looked very familiar. As we talked, each of us realized that we had crossed paths several times while living in the South and they even knew my brother Lil Kitt. These two guys were biological brothers. The older one called himself the Head Doctor, Numero Uno. We called him 'Doc'. He named his brother the Preacher Man, so we called him 'Preacher'.

After the movie they dropped me off at home. On the way there I told them that my brother would arrive in California the first week in June. I let them know that I was a barber and I did fantastic work so come see me. The very next week Preacher and his cousin Swede came and got their hair cut, and as promised I put a new style on both of them. Appreciatively, the next visit Preacher brought other cousins, but Doc, was a 'no show'. After friends and relatives continued to compliment Preacher and his cousins on how good their haircuts looked, Doc finally dragged his black behind in for a haircut. I am proud to say that the new hair style changed his whole appearance; he liked it, and the ladies just loved it.

These guys became my regular customers and my clientele grew. By means of those guys I met new people and in turn they became my clients also. Building my business became a little easier. For one reason everyone could see I had my own regular clients and I no longer seemed so desperate. Now it appeared that my customers were so pleased with my work, others wanted to be a part of this new experience.

Doc decided he would do something that would highlight my personality that would stay with me for days to come. He gave me a new name, 'The Cat'. This name had a bit of humor to it, especially the way Doc said it. Soon the girls started referring to me as 'The Cat' and the name became well-known. I was able to use a little of my creativity and designed a business card. The slogan was — "You've tried the rest why not try the best, "The Cat".

Picture for Barber license

I then took my barber's license down and removed the original approved State Board picture and replaced it with a 3"x5" picture resembling the one on my business card with the title "The Cat" engraved near the bottom center of the barber's license frame, and hung it adjacent to my chair. You would not believe the attention that little bit of confidence brought to me. Just that little card said more about me than I could ever say about myself. I believe this was the first time I began to find myself in the real world. Whenever my name came up, Doc would tell everyone that he made me. In fact, his exact words were, "I made The Cat". I must admit, Doc and the fellas proved to be my best allies. Progress did not come without complications, I was still walking. Sometimes on Friday the guys would wait until I finished for the evening and would drop me off at home. Doc and the Preacher had this bad black 1965 Corvair Spider convertible with bucket seats, stick shift with four in the floor. Doc was the owner, nonetheless Preacher was the driver and soulful at that. The Spider was equipped with a nice little record player and Doc just loved playing the record called "Soul Sauce" and there was still enough room for the girl to sit on the hump between the buckets, depending on the size of her bucket. I have to admit that Doc's ol' lady at that time had one on her. Doc wasn't short but she was at least two or three inches taller than him. She was super nice and quite shapely as well.

It had been almost a year, and during that time an astounding number of people have moved to South Central. This necessitated a decision by the Red Line to extend their hours of service. The latest hour for the northeast run was ten o'clock p.m. and this would put the South Central people in Watts about ten thirty-five p.m. at that point all services shut down to the ground.

The older barber Mr. Washington observed the metamorphosis of The Cat. My confidence, (something I didn't have to pray for) aggressiveness, style of speech, display of character and the way I jived around with the customers drawing them into conversations. Of course when my back was turned, he tells Jean, "Ms. Jean, you may not know this, but The Cat doesn't think his feet stank." Nevertheless he gave me his words of wisdom anyway. "My boy, he says, they are out to get you, and when I tell you they are out to get you, they are going to get you, you ain't no iron man. You know Sampson was a strong man, but when that woman started rubbing on him, he had to give it up, he told her where his strength was. Betta get out there and have yourself some fun. All I say is be careful. "Betta wear a rain coat." Another thing, you know them men that wear them hard hats and handle them tools that jump up and down, breaking up concrete? Hey, they're some tough men, but when they finish work, they go home to a woman."

Being genuinely dedicated to building my business I blew him off by saying, "Mr. Washington, I am not ready for that kind of action. I don't even have a ride."

Mr. Washington said, "Your home boys got rides, get with them."

Even though my business was growing, the needs of a poor man are so many. First of all, I was paying the shop owner thirty percent commission on everything I made. At two dollars a head I needed to cut a whole lot of heads to come out financially a winner. There was also self-employment tax at the end of the each year. I had no medical, vision, dental, nor even a pension plan. If something unexpected happened, I would have been in big trouble.

There is an advantage for women in this business verses men. In most cases a woman already has an old dude taking care of her and practically all the money she makes is free and clear. A man in this business, is not as fortunate, but what the heck? I am only nineteen. It won't hurt me to catch Ol' Red just a little while longer.

My conversation with Mr. Washington was about mid-week; I had a couple of nights to sleep on it. Friday, two days later, while on my way to work, I decided to hop off Ol' Red about half way and do some long overdue, but well deserved, shopping in the Florence area to reward myself with a pair of slacks and two shirts. I even wore the slacks out of the store. As coincidence might have it, getting off the Metro bus, to my ultimate surprise I spotted one of my home girls, Patricia Fox and quiet as it is kept, she is a natural fox. I recognized her right away because she always had a shape that fit a momma. As the guys back home say, 'she's a bad mamma jamma.'

"Pat Fox, is that you?" I asked.

"Yes, it's me."

"How long have you been in California?"

"Over a year", was her reply. "Melvin Rea I didn't know you were coming out here. Hey, we could have ridden out together."

"That really would have been something, wouldn't it? Pat, where do you live now?" I asked.

"Over on 58th and Budlong. Where are you living Katt?"

"Well, I live in Watts with my Aunt and cousin."

"I bet you have a whole lot of girlfriends since you've been out here.

"No, no I don't. I don't have time to mess around with these little crazy girls," was my response.

"Why don't you come over to see me sometime?"

"Ok, I'll do that."

"What are you doing tomorrow night," asked Pat.

"Oh, shucks, tomorrow night, I will most likely be working late. Unfortunately, on Saturdays I don't get home until about ten o clock"

"What about Sunday evening? Let's say about 7:30 p.m."

"That will be fine. So it's a date and I won't be late. By the way let me give you one of my business cards."

"Oh," says Pat, "a signature business card, I like that. That's cute."

With eyes slowly roving about, she says to me "Boy, you sure look good in those tight pants."

"Oh girl, we'll talk about that Sunday night."

"Alright, I'll see you then."

I got to work about noon that day and my customers were waiting. I apologized by saying 'I had a little problem with my connection today'. Everyone in the shop cracked up including Mr. Washington. I finished the work week and Sunday was a good day. Oh, the mood was so right, California sunshine, birds were chirping, a slight breeze from the ocean, airplanes on their decent to LAX, and the weather was just perfect. I groomed myself as I moved and hummed to an imaginary beat.

I was feeling so good, until I heard this familiar voice. "Where do you think you are going?

"I am going to see an old friend from Texas."

"Is it a girl or boy", asked Lil Aunt?

"It's a girl", was my reply.

"I tell you one thing, you better be back here no later than twelve o'clock mid-night. You hear me?"

Defiantly, I acknowledged Lil Aunt with an "Ok". At 4:31 p.m. I left walking down 92nd Street to catch the bus. After transferring several times and traveling on foot for a few blocks, I arrived at Pat's house on time. I must say it was nice being entertained, but having to be back at Lil Aunt's no later than mid-night did not leave me much time to visit.

Sad to say I had to leave Pat's at 9:00 o'clock because buses ran so seldom at that time of the evening on week-ends and I could not afford to miss that red bus. With the surge of energy I had just generated I probably could have walked from one end of the line to the other. Pulling the cord to stop the bus I got off at Vermont and began walking toward Vernon looking back for the bus as I walked.

Out of nowhere cruised a 1964 Malibu, canary yellow, black interior, pulling to the curb as the FM stereo played softly. "Hey, you want a ride?

"Yep"

"Hop in. Where are you going?" The dude asked.

My reply was, "down to Vernon. This sure is a bad ride," I commented.

"Oh, it's alright", he says.

"This is exactly the kind of car I always wanted. I just dig the canary yellow."

"Oh, it's not hard to get," he says. "Where have you been?"

"I went to see my girl friend."

"Did she turn you on?"

I go, "yeah."

"Why don't you turn me on?"

"Huh, huh, what did you say?" I asked.

"I said why don't you turn me on?"

I almost jumped out of my skin. That scared the crap out of me. I was as green as a persimmon sprout. It was a frightening thought, the guy could have pulled a gun on me and drive out somewhere in the boonies, but apparently this wasn't his intent.

Trying not to appear too shocked or embarrassed, I calmly said, "I don't play that." "You are just being modest. I bet you got a big one", he said.

"Naw, naw I'm not into that type of thing. I tell you what; let me out at the next corner." "Oh, don't get puffy daddy," he said and pulled to the curb.

After landing on solid ground the Cat made a decree: "I will never get into another Malibu unless it's my own." I arrived home at 10:45 p.m., glancing at the clock I felt relieved knowing that I didn't have to battle with the old ax.

"Well mister, how was your date?" asked Dottie.

"When does a man get some privacy around here?"

"I thought I would stay up to see how you like being out. Why didn't you stay out longer? You know you are your own man now."

"No thanks Dottie, you would be the very one to help set my bags outside."

"Since you must know, I had a very nice time at Pat's even if it did take me all night to get there. I spoke with her mother and she is also nice, although I didn't meet the husband. Now, on the way back this dude pulls up in this bad Malibu and gave me a ride. Come to find out he was a homosexual."

After listening to my little experience, Dottie busted out in laughter. "I told you, you didn't know what's happening. You were so infatuated over that car until you just got into that car without thinking. Country boy, you better learn this is not Texas." Just wait until I tell Lil Aunt.

"Hey, Dottie, don't tell her that. You know how she is."

"Oh yes, I am going to tell her."

"Dottie, I bet I'll never tell you anything again, because you talk too much." My plea went into one ear and out the other.

Her very words were, "*if you don't want it told, you should keep it to yourself.*"

By the next evening Lil Aunt had heard the news. Man! The gig was up.

"Yes, I have been waiting for you to get in from work. I want you to know I heard about you jumping into cars with sissies and caring on. Mister, you got one more time for something like that to happen and out you go."

"Oh, Lil Aunt, how was I supposed to know the guy was homosexual? I had no idea; the dude was a pink panther."

"You better know next time while you are out running around trying to court. Another thing while we are at it, you better be getting ready to help Junior, because he is going to be here week after next, and I mean you are going to help him too."

My reply was, "I'll do what I can, but I can hardly help myself."

"You will have to do something buddy boy."

The time passed by so fast it seemed as if only three days had passed by. After getting home from work Saturday night, I was greeted by none other than my brother Junior wearing a short quovadus hair style (Ivy League) and a thick mustache that looked like a big black hairy worm had crawled on his top lip and died. Junior was short in stature, even shorter than dad. His first question was, "Man, where are all the women?"

I attempted to set the record straight from the gate by saying, "Junior, that's a bad word in this shack. All these ol' bags want you to do is go to work, clean up and be sure you are in when mid-night strikes."

"I sure hope they don't think that they are going to make a housecat out of me," was Junior's rebuff.

"I'll tell you one thing Junior, Lil Aunt is tough as a boot. I'll show you around a little bit, but to tell you the truth man, I haven't got around very much myself, as you know I have been to barber school and now I am trying to build my business. I know a few dudes, but they don't get tight with you when you are from out of town and you don't have a car, baby you are on your own. What we can do tomorrow is catch the bus down town."

"Ok," says Junior.

While standing on the bus stop I saw several guys I knew riding past us with their girl friends.

"Junior, there is one thing you must know about city slickers. When those dudes are with their girl friends, they will act like they don't know you, or see you.

"Oh, Mister, let them pass, you don't need friends like that anyway", was Junior's thinking.

"Let me tell you this, on the 4th of July we were all at the park playing ball, and I asked this chick who lived on the next street could I walk her home. She says to me, "I don't want to walk, I am riding with Tony."

All I could say was 'ride on baby.' Of course, I couldn't blame her for that. What I need is some wheels. I guarantee you Junior, if I had any kind of old raggedy car I wouldn't have enough room for them to sit. Now the girls seem to like me, but the guys are downright chicken mess. I have devised a plan that will be the envy of any man. I will continue to save my money, fly to Detroit and pay cash for a bad ride I won't have to hide."

"Hey, Junior, I almost forgot, there are some home boys out here from Homer, Louisiana and all of them are related. Guess what? The good news is they are all coming in this Friday for their hair cuts. I will tell you how to get to the shop."

Sure enough we had a heck of a reunion at the barber shop. I had a lot of hair to cut that night including my brother's hair.

The next weekend Doc picked me and my brother up and carried us to a party where all the Motown sounds were played. If there was a party in town or out of town, Doc knew about it. After being in each other's company for sometime Doc named my brother Lil Caesar, and he strengthened that name by calling himself, 'Lil Caesar the woman squeezer.'

Doc has now established an organization that he called the Doctors. Each of us had a nick- name. What was so unique about this group was that practically all of us were southerners. The names Doc chose, were probably indicative of that. Perhaps I should name a few: The first pet name on his roster following the Preacher's was The Serpent—The Beast—The Rabbit—The Wizard—The Rookie—Blu—X—John the Baptist—Big Time—Earl the Pearl, who later became Lil Caesar's brother-in-law, and of course, yours truly, The Cat.

I tell you Doc was the glue of the group. When he calls to tell of a party his famous words were, "be there or be square." Lil Caesar was the cha-cha man. It was Bateman's Hall in Lynwood where Caesar first got loose doing his thing to Wes Montgomery's, "Bumping on Sunset". All the girls spontaneously lined up like ants to do a one minute dance with him. The record had to be played more than once for all of them to have equal time to cha-cha with Lil Caesar. It was standing room only, he turned that place out. Oh, it was so crowded on the floor, a fat girl stepped on The Katz's toe. Lil Caesar had so much soul, he had some left over, without a doubt Lil Caesar was one tired little brother when he finally finished dancing with all those women. The head doctor was on a leave of soul the night Lil Caesar took over. I did a great impression of Jackie Wilson and Soul Brother #1, James Brown. Of course everyone was on the floor for the slow drags. I stole my slow dance step from the Preacher and added to it a great deal of funk, (a mannish little step) becoming famous for that funky move. Without a doubt, Doc was the daddy of the Dip. Any girl who dipped with Doc for the first time was in for a surprise. When he went into his low reverse swing dip the girl came up riding high on Doc's left thigh.

The Serpent did his thing as everyone watched him do the Twine; nevertheless all the guys loved dancing with the one Doc called Pretty Little Miss Motown. I suppose all of us were unique in something, but The Beast was the boldest of us all, however, Doc claimed that The Baptist was bad from his beginning. Ms. Motown had a cute Lil'friend who answered to the name of Vicky Gee. She was sort of short in stature and had a gorgeous shape. When she did the Duck to "Sugar Pie Honey Bunch", and turned her back to the crowd, putting both hands on her hips and began wiggling her fingers, she owned the duck and the dance. I often wondered why Doc didn't give her a nick name. I suppose some things are just too beautiful to rename.

Lil Egypt was our mystery lady. Spontaneously, Doc would say, "Fellas, see Lil Egypt do the dance of the Pyramids." All of the doctors chimed in, "She walks, she talks, and she even crawls on her belly like a reptile". After we gave each other high fives everyone in earshot of our voices laughed, but they had no idea what we were talking about. A party was not a party without Ms. Santa Ana and her two sisters, and visiting us often from the Bay Area was the sweet little Ms. Cup Cake. Black Beauty was gracefully stacked, but light on her feet, nonetheless. I dare not omit Ms. Cadillac, Bertha and the one Lil Caesar calls Big Ann. Of course, The Wizard called her Cotton Candy. Ms. Cadillac was really something else, somewhat glamorous, she drove a Fleetwood Cadillac and lived in a security apartment. She had the audacity to tell my sister, "I can put Katz's little T-Bird in my glove compartment." The Pearl claimed, "She's the hands that rock the cradle." Oh, I almost forgot Ms Special Delivery, but that's all I'm going to say about that. Nevertheless, Doc appointed himself to choose the last song for the night. It was always a slow one and almost everyone was able to choose their special girl.

Doc was sometimes a cold dude. At least some of the guys thought so. There was one particular time when The Rabbit was on vacation back in Georgia visiting his folks; Doc introduced me to The Rabbit's girl, Christine. She was very attractive, quite womanly, a real cutie pie and had a slight shadow of a mustache on her top lip. As Doc introduced us, looking over the rim of his glasses he says, "The Cat is one of the doctors." There was something about being one of the doctors that simply turned people on. In Doc's own little way he urged me on. You see, he wanted to see if I could get Christine's attention and burn The Rabbit in the process. Her smile was like a bolt of lightning (knock you off your feet) and I even walked the girl home, but had no idea that she was The Rabbit's girl. I tried describing her to Mr. Washington, but he gave me a nasty grin and goes, "Dang! Brother, what kinda woman is that"? Even though The Rabbit was a dapper little dude, by the time he got back home I had pretty much singed ol' brother Rabbit's hide. Feeling a little bad about what had happen I confronted Doc, "Why didn't you tell me Christine was The Rabbit's girl?" He never answered, but busted out laughing instead. I suppose that was a quick lesson in survival of the fittest.

The parties and trips to the barber shop were a temporary relief from other anxieties. Jean and Mr. Washington were just as happy to see Doc and the fellas as I was, because they knew the star of the team would brighten up their day. He had an amazing ability to embellish and conjure up colorful stories that was sometimes unimaginable. There was a young guy always hanging around the barber shop named Buttons Roy Lewis. Not a good looking kid at all, but he wanted to be one us so bad. Jean was curious and wanted to know if he was related to any of us. With an emphatic "no" Doc tells Jean, "one thing about Buttons, he's too young, he's mannish and wants to be like The Cat, there is no way I would give Buttons a license, we all would get sued for malpractice." Jean thought that was so funny, all of us had to laugh. When Doc's around it's obvious who's driving the bus. Doc was so mischievous; he kept something goin' on all the time. When most of us were together he always had something to say about the one who wasn't there. He waited just as good when he got into the chair to go into his antics.

Doc says to us, "Hey fellas, I got a bad report on one of my Doctors."

Everyone became silent. In unison everyone asked, "Who?"

Doc confessed, "I'm sorry to say, but it's the Wizard." As he paused, we listened intently. "One of the Wizard's old ladies, (Mother Nature) called me," he says, "and she told me that the Wizard can't kiss." (Doc had problems keeping secrets.) He goes on to say, "I am sick and tired of hearing these bad reports about my Doctors." He added, "The very next time I see the Wizard, I'm gonna grab him and see if he can really kiss." We laughed so hard, we practically blew the roof off. All of us could visualize Doc grabbing the Wizard and him struggling to brake free.

As I stood continuing to laugh, Doc said, "Cat, cut my hair." After Doc took his seat in the waiting area, he began to tell a joke some white boy had told him at work. He told us about a polly-parrot in the midst of a truck load of hens. All of a sudden the driver looked back and saw all of the hens walking. The polly-parrot said, "Hey girls, when you make up your minds, you can ride."

Caesar says, "Shut up Doc, so Cat can finish cuttin' my hair."

Lil Caesar seemed to be more aggressive in the job market, or maybe people liked his disposition better than mine. Through a friend, Caesar obtained employment with a linen company in Hollywood. This really gave the old girls something to talk about, putting the Cat down to the ground. Dottie gave Caesar a great deal of praise.

"I tell you that Junior is on the ball. He's only been out here three or four days and has gone out and got himself a job making decent money, while you are sitting around the barber shop talking trash. The next thing we know you will be telling us you are going to get married. If I had a daughter, a little punk like you couldn't give her the time of day. One thing about you boy, can't anyone tell you nothing, and you are talking about buying a Thunderbird, who do you think is going to finance it, with the little chicken change you are making? The only way you get a T-Bird is catch a dead bird and print a T on it."

"That's alright Ms. Dottie; I am three times twice the person you think I am. One day I am going to buy a car so long, it will take me a week to turn the corner and a week and a half to park it, and besides that, I will have plenty of money, people will be pleased to call me Mister Katt."

"Mister Katt? Dottie busted into laughter once again, darn near shaking the whole house. She then falls over the chair throwing her leg in the air.

"Lil Aunt, Lil Aunt, please come here." Lil Aunt runs from the kitchen with her shoe in her hand, as if she were ready for a fight.

"What's wrong?" Lil Aunt asked.

"Woo, Lil Aunt, you should hear what this young man just told me. Mister, you go ahead and tell her."

"I ain't thinking about you Dottie", was my reply."

"Alright, alright, I'll tell you. He, he, he said, he said, he said.

"Oh, stop laughing girl," says Lil Aunt, "and tell me what this boy said."

"He said that one day soon he is going to buy a T-Bird so long it will take him a week to turn the corner and it would take him a week and a half to park it."

Lil Aunt stood looking at me as Dottie continues to laugh.

"But check this out Lil Aunt; he also said that he will have plenty of money and everyone will be delighted to call him Mister Katt."

Lil Aunt immediately falls into the other big chair busting into laughter. Her leg goes up in the air too, but not as high as Dottie's. Strange thing about Lil Aunt, she had the opportunity to see my business cards, examine the motto, but wasn't in the lease impressed. In fact, in her eyes I was still just a boy.

My Fridays were long days and my evenings were just as demanding. Catching the Red bus on the days the fellas wasn't in, was wearing me out. When I finally got home my first stop was the sofa in the den, in front of my room where I would fall asleep, only to be disturbed by Lil Aunt.

"Get yourself up from here and go to bed."

"Huh

"You heard me. Get yourself up and go to bed."As I wobbled to my room, Lil Aunt called out, "Just a minute sleeping beauty, I have a little something I want you to snooze on. If you don't do more cleaning around here, you will have to find you somewhere else to stay. I don't like you giving me sassy looks when I am talking to you. What I want you to do is to keep your rent for one month, and you decide whether or not you want to follow my rules. Now if you decide you don't want to, take the rent and get out. That will be my going away present."

Lil Aunt's little speech raised much enthusiasm. I started saving my rent and commenced hiding it under the kitchen stove. My display of humility was evident, as I promoted domestic hygiene in order to remain in the house.

It is truly amazing what crawls around in a person's mind. I never caused Lil Aunt problems by having girls in the house or any other things common with young men my age. I was more concerned with building my business, acquiring financial freedom and being respectful. These things were instilled in me by my parents. You see, I had the ability to talk, (probably too much, in the presence of the ol' girls) I was quite different when it comes to my brother Lil Caesar "the woman squeezer". The law of Lil Aunt was bound on him just as it was on me "Do not have any girls coming into this house."

Although, Caesar said he would not, on his days off, girls came over and spent most of the day with him. If Lil Aunt happened to come home early and proceed down the driveway, when approaching the back door, Caesar would send the girl out the front door, and that reminded me of no one other than my ol' man. The old battle ax didn't even have a clue. Caesar has always been a character; when we were growing up everywhere he went, he met new girls. We didn't have a telephone and when we got one, Dad only on occasions, allowed us to make a local phone call, otherwise we had to resort to communication by mail. I hated washing dishes and Caesar wasn't such a great student, therefore I consented to writing letters to Caesar's girl friends if he would take care of the dishes for me. I consulted him to find out what he wanted me to tell each girl. He responded by saying, "Just tell them all the same thing."

Through all of this, something good happened as well as something bad. On Wednesday, August 11, 1965, the Watts riot broke out. Reporters referred to this situation as 'Hell in the City of Angels'. On that momentous day a white Los Angeles policeman on a motorcycle pulled over an African American, named Toby Frost, who someone reported was driving drunk. When the policeman caught sight of him driving down the street they pulled him and his brother over for questioning and shortly afterward Frost's mother, Annie, arrived on the scene. A crowd of onlookers began to taunt the policeman. A second officer was called in. It was this officer who began whaling his baton on the crowd. Police used their batons to subdue Frost and his brother resulting in the arrest of all three family members. Shortly after that the police left, tensions brewed and rioting began, burning and looting with the slogan, 'burn baby burn', and it lasted five days. Jean had many clients who lived in South Central and knew the Frost family personally, but each of them had a slightly different version of what really went down.

City officials initially blamed outside promoters for the uprising, although studies showed that the majority of participants had lived in Watts all of their lives. It was also learned that protester's anger was directed primarily at the white storeowners in the neighborhood and at members of the all white Los Angeles Police Department.

Conservative whites viewed the uprising as a symbol of the aggressive move of Civil Rights. In those days they blamed everything on Civil Rights. Most of the damages from the riot were confined to the businesses that had caused tension in the area because of unfairness. Homes were not the target but some caught fire due to close proximity. It is believed that the real cause for the Watts riot was police brutality, high unemployment rate, poor schools, and inferior living conditions among other things.

I was at work that Wednesday standing outside of the shop when I saw two black guys in a black '56 Bel Aire convertible chasing whitey. One of them was standing and reeling from side to side as he threw cans of beer at whitey as he moved swiftly away from them. Whitey got away simply because he was driving a better car than the brothers. A few minutes later the same two black dudes came back down the street with their old car smoking like a pine-top.

Now the good thing --- Jean says to me, "Katt, they are rioting out there, all over South Central, you can't go home; all the buses have stopped running. Do you have anyone you can stay with?" "Oh yes, my sister lives not for from here."

"That's good", said Jean, "and I will take you over there after work and you call me tomorrow before you come to work."

In the mean time Jean sprayed the words soul sister on her store front windows in order for her shop to be spared. I stayed with my sister and brother-in-law for the rest of the week. During that time we discussed Lil Aunt and Dottie. My brother-in-law, who we called Blu suggested that I continue to live with them because it would be more covenant and close enough to walk to work if necessary. Besides that, I would not have to suffer the humiliation by Lil Aunt and Dottie. Now that made a lot of sense to me, after all, Lil Aunt had already given me an ultimatum.

This was not a difficult decision for me at all. Sunday was the last day of the rioting; the National Guard had everything under control. I called Doc and Preacher called me. Preacher came over and picked me up. We traveled to Watts and got my things while

Lil Aunt was at church. Of course I had very little to get. It took us less than five minutes to get my stuff and I was dropped off at my sister's house, and the chapter of my life with Lil Aunt and Dottie was now closed.

During those days prior to the riot, the number one radio station blasting the air waves was KGFJ. The favorite disc-jockey was The Magnificent Montaque. He kept his listeners fired up by playing all of the soulful Motown sounds. When he came on the air he would say, "This is The Magnificent Montaque baby---- wake up Los Angeles and burn." The Fans calling in were saying, "This is so-and-so, I weigh 110 pounds and I am brown all year round." Montaque says, "Have mercy baby, burn baby burn."

Since the rioters were using the slogan "burn baby burn", authorities began to investigate The Magnificent Montaque to ascertain whether or not he was inciting the riot. Consequently, their findings were not consistent with their suspicions. Nevertheless, the slogan "burn baby burn" was instantly rebuked and suspended by Montaque. He now inserted a new phrase in his arsenal of soul, "Learn baby learn". It wasn't long at all after things cooled down that The Magnificent Montaque left the air waves.

I had the opportunity to visit the Shrine auditorium in West Los Angeles to witness Montague's Farewell and concert. There were more soul celebrities in one place then I had ever seen in my life. Rudy Ray Moore was the master of ceremonies. He introduced Little Richard as the Tooty Fruity Man. Little Richard came out bare-footed and showing his bare chest with a pair of designer slacks on and said, "I know you think this is a wig I have on, but this is my own lovely head of hair." He stole the show when he sang "Tooty Fruity" and "Good Golly Ms Molly". Chuck Berry just had to do his little duck walk. I don't recall if B.B. King was there or not, but Red Foxx was there lying and smoking up a fog. It's always refreshing to hear Gladys Knight and Etta James. There were so many stars there I can barely remember. Everyone stood on their feet when Marvin

Gaye did his little thing to "Hitch Hike". Solomon Burke closed the show when he sang "Keep the Light Burning in the Window until I Get Home."

There was something that puzzled me to no end, when making my departure from Lil Aunt's. When Preacher took me to get my things, I couldn't find my money that I was hiding under the stove. I later found out that Caesar told Lil Aunt that I had intentions of leaving and that I had been saving my money under the stove. I suppose he thought I had taken the money with me. I automatically decided at that point that Caesar was just like Big Poppa (Dad's father) he couldn't keep nothing.

CHAPTER FOUR

Round Two

BARBERING NEVER DID RETURN back to normal. We are now experiencing a new era of Black Power and the expression of the Afro. Most of the young guys went Afro and seldom got it lined or shaped. That really complicated things for a relatively new barber. Nevertheless, I met new people by way of my sister. I met an older man who most everyone called Batman, but I referred to him as Bat. He became like a father to me, and better yet, he became one of my clients.

I could ask him just about anything in confidence and I could take it to the bank. Bat had many years of experience and had acquired much wisdom. I can assure you that Bat's experience and advice was invaluable. In fact, he was Big Time's father. Bat showed me the ritzy scenes of Los Angeles, Beverly Hills, Redondo Beach, and other places a mature person would enjoy. At the same time, I would keep in touch with my home boys who had given me great support.

Even though business had made a sudden turn south, I saved every penny possible because I knew if I was going to stand out and be perceived as different, I needed some new rags and a nice ride I would not have to hide. I felt comfortable talking to Bat, so I began to lay it all out as to what I thought I needed to shine.

Bat says to me, "Hey, Katt, man, I understand you want a sharp ride, having all the girls running after you, but let me tell you something, those fine cars will break you. Insurance, car notes, and the upkeep will kill you. You won't even have enough money left to buy those gals a soda cracker. Man, why don't you get yourself a nice little transportation car just to keep from walking? I will even help you find one. Now if you see something you might like, let me know and we will go and check it out. By the way, don't look for anything in nigger's-ville, because it's already worn out. Go out in the valley where the white folks live, by-gum, I bet you'll find a good one out there. Another thing, in the mean time, you start buying yourself some mean threads and those other cats won't be able to touch you. I know just the place, let's go down town next Monday and I will introduce you."

"*Murray's*" down town was a very nice store. Tailor-made suits and other sharp men's apparel; dress shirts with French cuffs and the like. *Murray's* required a down payment on a lay-a-way plan, cash or credit card. Of course I chose the lay-a-way plan and the Cat was on his way. Now, I can get decked for days. The next Monday I caught a bus to Van Nays, California and departed on Van Nuys Boulevard where car dealerships was king, at least for a quarter of a mile. I walked the south side of the street and back down the north side until I spotted a clean little sky blue 1960 Rambler advertised for $399.00.

I returned home and called Bat. The next day Bat and I went to check it out. He assured me it was a nice little vehicle and it should last a long time if I take good care of it. Bat co-signed for me with the agreement not to tell Big Time or anyone else. We wrapped everything up and headed for home. Oh boy, now I have some wheels and I can go as I please, thanks to Bat. Wining and dining has now become my weapon of choice.

What nice young lady wouldn't rather be sitting near a bay window on the ocean in some lavish restaurant having a fabulous dinner and sipping some Chablis while others are sitting on hard benches watching the fellas play football? People always gave me an inquisitive look when the reservationist called out, "Mister Katt, reservation for two". I knew she would barely touch her lobster after eating their house salad, Caesar salad, or combination salad as they prepared it before her eyes. She never ordered drinks, but modestly sipped on mine as I had politely placed the freshly poured glass of vintage in front of her lips. I, now move in for the kill. I kindly suggested she take the leftovers and let her brother taste them. I was genuinely happy because just as I thought she gave them to her mother instead.

It worked just fine, I won, I couldn't do no wrong. I never suggested stopping by Jump-N–Jack motel, oh, no, I would never do that. I have never been quite that naughty. Sometime later I insisted she invite her mother to join us for dinner. From that day forward the Cat became a protected species. With my new success I quit football outings and took up dining and girls. (The Crop of America, Sugar and Spice and everything nice.)

In the meantime and between times, whenever Doc or the fellas came by or called to inform me of a party, I could be there, and not be square. Ten thirty was my E. T. A. for the parties because of working late. Of course others thought I was purposely bringing attention to myself. Late or not I was always sharp as-a-tack. Of course, I took a little teasing from Doc, because of being so sharp, he said that after the parties I had to go jump into a little turtle looking car.

Needless to say I worked eighteen months under Jean as a licensed barber. I applied and took the examination for my Master Barber's license. My endeavor was successful and my commission decreased by five percent.

I am sure that every little bit helps, but not enough to brag about. During this time Caesar had changed his employment from Hollywood to Huntington Park doing the same type of work. He bought lots of new clothes and a used car. It appeared that his savings was also intact. I was very happy for him. The good thing for me, I no longer lived in South Central and did not have to listen to Lil Aunt and Dottie's crap. Another good thing for Caesar, Dottie finally got married and moved out.

I honestly believe Bat's advice to purchase the Rambler was the appropriate thing to do because I was still able to save a little of my income. I barbered for another year and nine months and then I flew to Detroit and paid cash for a 1966 Thunderbird; black on black in black with a swing-a-way steering wheel. I drove to Washington D.C. where I visited my oldest sister and her husband Gorgeous George. From there, to Maryland, Tennessee, Florida, Georgia, and Louisiana, and on to Texas to see Mom and Dad whom I hadn't seen since Dad had me to catch the first thing smokin'.

They were delighted to see me although things hadn't changed very much. Dad had made some progress in the cattle business. His Black Angus cattle really looked good, but I could see that he still needed a little help. I promised the old man I would help him out whenever I could. Two weeks away from the city was enough for me, so I headed back to the West Coast.

After being back in California for a few months I began to realize what Bat said about the larger cars was definitely correct. I tell you, that T-Bird was much more expensive to maintain. The insurance cost much more on the T-Bird than the Rambler and everything else. Really a larger car is somewhat like an alligator; it will eat you alive, although I sure did look good and felt important riding in that bad black T-Bird.

After owning this car for some time I began to realize I had not yet reached the pinnacle of success. The Cat just had to face reality; I was not making enough money. It was time to put a move on Lil Caesar. I felt I could do this now; after all, my ego was significantly smaller. I invited him over for a chat.

My words to Caesar were, "Man, I can't make it at the barber shop. I am not making enough money; no benefits and probably not taking out enough for social security either. You know the girls like me, but what can I do for them? Nothing! Caesar this is getting to be for the birds. Hey, Caesar, do you think maybe you can get me a job where you work?"

"I tell you what Cat, I will talk with the man Monday and I will get back with you." "Okay Caesar, thanks, do what you can."

With Caesar's help I had no problem getting hired. I started work the very next day.

"Well what are you going to do about barbering?" Caesar asked.

"Well, I will go to the shop after I get off from the laundry and also work weekends."

On this job, the main attraction of the day was Lil Caesar at lunch time when the 'roach coach' rolled up. Lil Caesar walked out with his boom-box on his shoulder. As soon as he hears one of his favorite Motown songs by Steve Wonder, "I was made to love her." He sat his box down and threw himself to the ground and did the alligator. As expected, everyone laughed and clapped for Caesar.

I worked in the laundry and cut hair part time for another year and nine months. Money was no longer a problem. I bought several new suits, some of the finest tailor-made suits that money could buy along with the accessories to match. At this point in my life I honestly believed that clothes made the man, and to look good is to feel good.

Doc and the fellas had no jealousy what-so-ever; they continued to get their hair cuts on Friday evenings and on certain occasions early Saturday morning. Sad to say, that Big Time was something else. He was a Californian and ooh, how Big Time thought his stuff was so tight. He was big and tall and he talked big with somewhat of a lofty vocabulary.

One Friday evening unlike any other evening the fellas came in while I was cutting Big Time's hair. Maybe I shouldn't have been surprised, but Big Time showed his natural butt. He contended that I wasn't cutting his hair right. He immediately jumps up like a maniac and jerks the chair cloth off forcing the metal neck clip to hurt my little finger. Not only did he embarrass me but the entire organization as well. Jean walked over to Big Time, chastising him by trying to shame him for his actions.

She lays her big finger on his shoulder and tells him, "Cat is your friend. You don't do that to a friend."

Trying to shame Big Time was like putting lipstick on a pig. Clearly he should have conceded, but didn't even show a twinge of guilt. If we ever had doubts about him, now we know, "Big Time is bad news." It is my knowledge that Big Time has always been contentious. What he failed to understand was, you can shear a sheep several times but you can only skin him once. As time passed we pretended that everything was a-okay, but I am sure that Big Time could feel the chill. Big Time and he alone had this thing about trying to catch the rest of us into stuff. He really wanted to catch The Cat disturbing the peace, but could never pick up my scent. Big Time couldn't catch a Cub Scout.

Sometime later after things had cooled down, Jean talked to me as I expected an experienced woman would. When she did speak to me, she goes on to breakdown Big Time's pedigree.

She said, "Big Time is not your friend. He's jealous of you. You see, he's married and have a baby and can't do like you. Those other guys are your friends."

Lil Caesar was in the shop one Friday evening when the fellas were there and they began telling Caesar how Big Time lost his cool.

Caesar asked, "Did Big Time do that Cat?

I didn't say a word.

Doc says, "Cat you know he did, ask Jean."

Everyone in the shop concurred that it did happen.

Becoming irate by Big Time's indiscretion Caesar goes, "I wish I had been here, I ain't like Cat. "I'll kick Big Time's a--". Everyone in the shop cracked up, including Jean. Prior to this discussion I never told Caesar about Big Time's little capper because I knew he had a temper.

I was told that Lil Aunt was annoyed with Caesar playing his radio too loud, as he was ironing his shirts and jamming to "Poppa was a rolling stone". Lil Aunt, without a word marched right passed him, took his radio and threw it to the concrete floor and shattered it to pieces. The last words Caesar remember the song saying was--"when he dieeeeeed." He responded by pushing her down on the bunk bed. I thought for sure Caesar would have gotten thrown out by his mustache, but she allowed him to stay.

Finally late one Friday evening, Caesar was able to catch up with Big Time in his usual position, in my chair.

Lil Caesar said, "Yeah, Big Time, I heard about you showing your big a--in this shop." Caesar took both of his fists and did a very quick, ratta tat-tat on Big Time's thigh and Big Time jumped straight up.

All of the fellas (our soul patrol) sprung to their feet, they go, "No, no, um-um Big Time, we ain't having that." He knew it was best to retreat; therefore he slowly eased his big behind down in the chair.

The strangest of things happened while working at the laundry. Caesar was instrumental in getting me the job, but after a period of time he was laid off and they kept me working. It had something to do with losing a contract with Camp Pendleton. He was called back to work but meanwhile Doc got him a job where he worked. Thanks to Doc he really looked out for the fellas.

There is something about me you probably don't know. It could be heredity. Sometimes good just isn't good enough. I no longer had money problems, but that job at the laundry just didn't fit my character. Sticking my head in and out of those huge tumblers, pulling out those steamy shirts caused perspiration from my head and face to drip like mad.

This wasn't cool for the Cat; I needed something a lot less sweaty. If not a white collar job, at lease a collar that wouldn't get soaking wet with sweat. Something else that really wee-weed me off about that job was Mario, the supervisor. While I was busy pulling those hot clothes from the tumbler, Mario would so often be standing behind me from a short distant with his legs crossed watching me work. When I turn around and saw him, he would split like he had just got scalded by hot water; oh, he hauled behind alright.

Because of the Affirmative Action Program, my brother-in-law Blu was the first black man to be hired on at one of the major oil companies of Southern California. Of course, my sister was afraid for him because he was the only black person working there. This was a blue collar job quite a ways out on Broadway. The only requirement for the job was good health and a high school diploma. This opened a new avenue for blacks to earn a decent income.

I lived with my sister and Blu for several more months and I received a telephone call. Mom had another older sister who resided in Los Angeles on the west side also known as the best side. She was always cool and calm, her disposition was nothing like Lil Aunt's, but closely resembled my mother's. We affectionately referred to her as Aunt E, unfortunately, a bit of senility had set in; of course, that was the reason for the phone call. My cousin Tee and her husband had moved out near the ocean to the Rolling Hills Estates. Cousin Tee felt it was not wise for Aunt E to live alone. She wanted to know if I would consider living with Aunt E, to keep an eye on her and I would not be required to pay rent.

I jumped at the opportunity. Now, I would have my own bedroom and practically all the privacy a young man would need and besides that, traveling across town to work wasn't a problem because gasoline was only thirty-three cent per gallon. This move across town was a boost for my ego. When someone would ask where I lived, I would proudly say on the west side. I kept in close contact with my sister; in fact, I ate dinner with her and the family most of the time after work. Blu came to the conclusion that I would probably be working continuously for someone for the rest of my life, so why not work for a company that offers great benefits and substantial income. He admonished me to apply for employment where he worked.

I took his advice and within sixty days personnel called to see if I was still interested in the job. Aunt E took the call; I must say I was thoroughly surprised that she remembered to tell me. The company scheduled me for a physical with the staff doctor and I passed the physical with flying colors. The doctor said I looked like a stud on the tread mill. I was asked whether or not I would be available for work February the 9th? I responded by saying, that will be fine.

When I reported for work at the LA terminal the strangest of things was going on. The workers were on strike. Apparently the union steward was the only one walking the picket-line. He did this only half of the day and returned to work the remainder. The steward's assistant now walked the line the rest of the day. What a joke!

The irony of it all was that the company brought in two trailers. One was for catering and the other for sleep-over. Free meals were prepared three times a day for the office staff and especially for the warehousemen who wanted to keep working during the so-called strike.

I also noticed that at twelve o'clock the union steward immediately left the picket-line and joined the rest of us in the trailer for lunch.

I was really baffled at what I saw; I asked Blu, "Say, wasn't that dude out walking the picket line?"

Blu said "Yeah, that's the way they do things around here. Just enjoy your food."

I was assigned to the accessory warehouse where we picked and packed auto parts to be shipped out to the company's service stations throughout Southern California. This was probably one of the best non-skilled jobs a young black man could find. As the old cliché has it…it was being in the right place at the right time.

I was on probation for six months and after that ended I began to accumulate sick days with pay. After being with the company for a year I was financially able to purchase any vehicle I ever dreamed of owning. I worked for another six months and traded the T- Bird in on a new Cadillac and reserved a set of personalized environmental license plates that read, "Mr. Katt".

Now, there were things said about me I do not want to repeat. The fellas continued to refer to me as The Cat, but to others I was commonly known as Katt or Mister Katt.

1974 Cadillac Coupe de Ville

I continued to work in accessories for at least another year and a half. Day after day things had now become monotonous. I suppose we could say the Katt had out grown his cage. I began to say to myself, "With a company this large, surely there must be something more challenging and exciting for me." I began to inquire at the local personnel office.

"Well, what do you want to do" was the question.

"I'm not really sure. What are some of the other jobs that are available?"

"There are a number of positions associated with this company, but, I would think you would not want something that would require a college degree. Am I correct?"

"Yes you are correct."

"What do you think about becoming a sales representative?"

"Tell me a little about the responsibility."

"You are very well familiar with the accessories. The sales Rep. makes sure the service station owners are purchasing their products from the company. You will receive a company car to check on these guys. First of all, you will try your hand at taking orders from the code-a-phone. These are the orders you are now filling in the warehouse. You think you would like to try that?"

"Oh, I sure would."

"Ok, I will pass this on to the terminal supervisor."

Just a few days later the terminal supervisor called me in for a chat. He assured me that the company needed more competent sales reps and since I had done such a fantastic job in accessories he would give me the opportunity to become a sales representative. This was not going to be so easy because the next day I would have to start work at 5 o'clock in the morning while most of the workers were still in bed. The reason for this ungodly hour was to ensure that orders would be available when the accessory workers clocked in. I was obligated to perform this task until all orders were completed and then go to the warehouse for the rest of the day.

To my surprise there were so many foreigners operating the stations I could barely complete a single order. The ratio was about 6 to 1. I felt we had just been invaded by Peking. I was totally frustrated. The owners would say something like this, "Chen, lease 2-2-4-2 PF yum-yum chop-chop. I finally interpreted that to mean he wanted a case of PF 2 oil filters. I was given a pat on the back and assurance that things would get better. A week and a half had passed by and I still didn't feel comfortable, so I decided to return to the warehouse full time.

I didn't feel that I had failed, perhaps sales wasn't for the Katt. During the next three months I noticed the outside truck drivers as they came in to pick up products and our truck drivers going out to deliver. I began to take a serious look at distribution. After conversing with two of the black truck drivers at LAT I was thoroughly convinced, I can do this job.

I made an appointment to meet with the terminal superintendent of transportation. He told me, "You are certainly a very good worker, but you might be a little small as a truck driver."

"Yeah, I'm a little piece of leather but, I am well put together."

"Okay," he laughed. "I like that. I will give you a shot at becoming a trucker.". "I sure do appreciate that sir," I nodded.

"Don't thank me yet", he says, "You have to wait your turn. There are other guys ahead of you and you will not be treated any differently from the rest. You will also take whatever shift that is available, day or night."

While anxiously waiting for the opening I asked Jimenez, who transferred from accessories before me, how did he like trucking? He told me, "it's good", in fact, he said "its real good." You should come over and join us."

CHAPTER FIVE

Round Three

IT SEEMED AS IF my name would never be called as I anxiously awaited that moment. Mid-way through the afternoon work schedule the shop foreman tells me that I need to see Dick Tyree in the driver's dispatch room. I go over to see Mr. Tyree. He was sort of a chunky fella and wore his pants a few inches above his waist. He was bald on top, although father time had reserved most of his sides and side burns. Dick informed me that Monday morning I would start training to see if I could cut the mustard (To see if I was suitable to drive). If I handled the assignment well enough I would then be in training for two weeks on the road. He gave me a weird stare as most white folks love to do. Wearing those big hoot-owl looking glasses, he tells me if I make the two weeks okay, then I would be classified as a permanent truck driver.

He introduced me to his assistant dispatcher Hank Terrell who I would report to during training. "You think you are going to like trucking' boy?" he asked.

"Yes, I sure think so, was my reply."

"Okay boy, check in with Hank on Monday morning at seven o'clock.

In view of the times, I definitely thought Dick used the word boy too loosely. I wasn't offended because there were all kinds of people coming into LAT for products, cross-country drivers, line drivers, owner-operators and the like.

Many of the drivers consisted of old southern pecker-woods. One day while still working in accessories we all headed to the room for afternoon break. Lots of trash talking goes on in a room like this. After a few jive words were laid down by the employees, one of the out-of-state drivers who was waiting for his truck to be loaded said, "By-God, we use to take them nigger shooters and shoot dogs in the butt with um."

"Everyone became quiet. The hush became even greater as he displayed his ignorance by repeating the same expression a second time. I suppose he finally realized that the comment wasn't nice, especially in a mixed crowd, because he changed his words from nigger shooter to sling shot as everyone starred him down.

Monday morning had finally come and Hank Terrell introduced me to Dick Thomas, the driver trainer. Mr. Thomas was a man of considerable height and also bald on top. With clip board in hand he asked for my driver's license and questioned my driving history. He then made a copy and handed the license back to me.

We walked to the south end of the terminal to the area where the contractor trucks were parked.

Those trucks in particular were tankers equipped with four separate compartments and a barrel rack in the rear. Dick's motto was '*safety always comes first*'. Therefore we began with the safety inspection. I was told to always walk around the truck and look for cracked or broken lens, check engine oil level and radiator before starting the engine. The next step after starting the engine is to turn on all lights and flashers. While the engine is warming up, walk around the truck and thump all tires with a tire tool to see if there are any flats. Next, check all signal lights to see if they are working properly. The last items on the list were very important, both horns must blow and the air-brakes when applied must hold one hundred eighty pounds of pressure for at lease one minute.

The trucks trade name was Diamond T. It had positive action, twin screw. The transmission had two stick shifts side by side.

The one on the left was the primary gear box with a four speed shift and on the right was the secondary gear box with a two speed shift which is also called the brownie.

That type of truck was a little complicated to operate because of its design. The stick shifts must be opposite of each other when changing gears. The trick was to move one shift up and the other one down almost simultaneously while double clutching. I have to admit that kind of maneuvering called for a little fortitude, but with an experienced instructor like Dick Thomas things went very well.

After several hours of intense training in the yard we retreated to the dispatch room. There we were greeted by Dick Tyree. "I bet it wasn't as easy as you thought it was huh, boy? I've seen a whole lot worse in my day", said Dick Thomas. "Well good, responded Mr. Tyree. From his attaché case Dick Thomas handed me a motor vehicle handbook to study as an aid to acquire a Class II driver's license.

"Oh, I will take care of this right away", I said.

"Oh, no", says Dick. "Take your time, study and pass the exam".

I said "no problem", as I quickly fanned through the pages.

"Tomorrow you will begin riding with Jimenez," says Dick Tyree. He gave me a special pair of work gloves but, no uniform.

"By the way, you must be here no later than six o'clock in the morning. In meantime don't forget to study your book."

"Right- On", was my reply. As I exited the room I over-heard them say, "You know I think he is going to be alright."

My first day out with Jimenez was exciting. I had the pleasure of seeing the areas of the rich and famous. He and I drove through Santa Monica touching the outskirts of 5th and Promenade and then to Pacific Coast Highway to Santa-Nez Canyon where we fueled heavy equipment used for new home construction. Santa-Nez Estate parallels the Pacific Coast Hwy, but the swanky area of Pacific Palisades overlooks the Coast Highway as well as the Pacific Ocean.

I rode with Jimenez for about a week and one day, during that time I said to him, "Hey, on your way to the Canyon this morning, drop me off on Exposition. I need to take the driver's written exam. Pick me up on your way back."

"If you are not outside when I come back," he said, "I will go ahead and reload and get you when I make the second trip."

"Okay, that's a deal."

The timing of the situation couldn't have been better. When Jimenez pulled up I was already standing at the curb smiling with exam papers in hand. "I take it that you passed the exam"? asked Jimenez.

"I sure did so, what did you expect from a cat like me?

"Good for you," was his reply.

I couldn't wait for Frank to park the truck. Hopping from the cab landing on both feet I immediately handed my Certificate of Completion to Hank.

"How did you manage that pussycat?

"Well, I took the examination while Jimenez was gone to the Canyon."

"You did what? As their eyes were on me, both Dick and Hank Terrell shook their heads and laughed. This was Hank's first time engaging in a conversation with me from day one. I wondered if he would ever talk. Nevertheless Jimenez and I worked together for another week and Hank asked whether or not I was ready to go on my own. With all the confidence in the world I responded by saying, "I am ready Teddy."

The next day I ran the route alone. Just like clock-work I was back in the terminal on time waiting for another load. At about five thirty a.m. the following morning I was loading my truck and to my surprise Dick Thomas approached the loading rack.

I said "Hey Dick what are you doing up so early?"

"I couldn't sleep".

Yeah, right, I said to myself. The truth about the matter was that he came to check me out. Dick watched me as I finished loading the truck.

"A word of caution," he says, "that meter won't get your feet wet." What he meant was to watch the compartment and not over fill it. That morning went very well for me. In fact it went so well Dick Thomas took the rest of the day off. I was so pleased that things were going right for me. I could not believe that within three short days things could go so very, very wrong. The contractor that we serviced in Santa Nez Canyon now had fifteen units of equipment at Los Angeles International Airport. Getting into LAX was a nightmare. After getting in I discovered there wasn't enough fuel on board to service all of the equipment. I could fix the fuel problem by leaving Santa Nez and go straight to LAT to refuel and then head for LA International.

That solved the fuel problem, but did not help my efficiency. The biggest hurdle wasn't fueling; it was getting in to fuel the equipment. I was not permitted to enter the runway on arrival. Outside trucks had to stop at the guard shack and wait for an escort, which sometimes took thirty minutes or more. It took a little more time because not all equipment was in the same location as it was in Santa Nez for home construction. Things didn't get much better because I had to be escorted back off the runway.

This put me back in LAT anywhere between noon and one o'clock in the afternoon because everyone in LA knows that lunch time traffic is a doozy. Evidently Hank must have complained to Dick Tyree about how long it was taking me to do the route. I was given an equipment disbursement pad to list all equipment numbers, time of service and how much fuel it took. Somehow I felt that Murphy's Law was in motion because the more I did what was asked of me, the less Hank understood why it took more time than expected to do the job.

I was somewhat surprised a few days later when I was cornered by Dick Tyree and my shop steward. Dick began to tell me it was taking too long to do my route, but he allowed me to explain the complexity.

"Dick when I took over this route the contractor only had equipment in Santa Nez Canyon. Now he has pieces of equipment strewn all over the airport and I have to wait at the gate for an escort and it takes forever to get in. To complicate matters there isn't enough fuel remaining to service the next stop. Therefore I have to return to the terminal to reload. Dick I tell you when I get out of LAX I am right in the midst of noon traffic and that's a real mother for ya."

Both men slightly grinned. "Did you tell Hank about this?

"Sure I did, I even filled out a distribution sheet, time of delivery and the whole nine yards."

Ok, well, do you want to go back to the warehouse? Oh, my spirit almost fainted away within me, as I stood crying from one eye. I am sure he asks that question so I would disqualify myself.

I knew in my heart, quitting was not an option. I must continue slugging it out. He goes on to say in a discouraging way, "you won't always be driving a fuel truck. The time will come when you will have to go on stake truck and those barrels weight over 500 lbs each."

I realized that this was not a time for the faint of heart; therefore I gained my composure while seeing my prosperity was being ripped apart. A person did not have to be a rocket scientist to know that going back to the warehouse would result in $2.50 less per hour and that is humiliating in itself. My answer was an emphatic "no."

This was the most crucial period of my career, but I remained absolute.

Dick Tyree now turned to the shop steward and said, "Chuck, the Katt is doing an excellent job handling the equipment, and we don't even have one customer complaint. I know he is trying hard to do a good job. I'll tell you what I am going to do. I am going to give him two more weeks."

He turns to me and says, "I am taking you out of West LA and the Canyon and giving you another route to see what you do with that. I will be on vacation for two weeks. When I come back I will ask Hank how you did."

"Oh, thank you Dick", was my reply.

"Ok, boy I will see you when I get back.

I now understood what my old man meant when he said *I would have to be twice as good as the white man in order to keep a job.*

Those words, two weeks were the most beautiful words I had ever heard. The only words that even came close were when Blu said, "You can live with us". I had no intentions of giving up this great opportunity. This was the only thing on my mine. Even if marriage was in my mind it had to be far in the back of it. With this extension granted by Dick Tyree, it looks like time was going to be the Katt's friend once again.

Without any further notice my route was changed from West LA to Long Beach. Giving me the Long Beach route was just like throwing the rabbit in the briar patch or putting the cat in the ally. This route included Long Beach, San Pedro, Terminal Island, Port of Call and then a short cut across Vincent Thomas Bridge to a road that winds its way to Signal Hill northeast of Long Beach.

Rolling Hills Estate, Redondo Beach and Marina Delray are the western beach towns. There were other small towns on the east which included municipalities. I knew I had to prove I was an expert and not a poot-butt. Therefore I had to really get to humping and those guys really had me humping! My first stop in the morning was Rolling Hills Estate, not very far from a mobile home park. Pacific Coast Hwy was the gateway to the beaches. Five-thirty in the morning Pacific Coast Hwy to Rolling Hills was practically wide open.

I had that truck singing a simple song. Within two blocks of my turn off I would drop a gear in the main box and decelerate. I tell you, that truck sounded like a siren going off. Whether foggy or clear, Jump-N-Jack neon sign on the right side of the Coast Highway was an identifying marker. Approaching the turn-in, I down shifted two more times and flipped the differential switch which caused one of the rear axles to slide over as it strutted up the hill past the mobile homes. Needless to say, the truck caused such a ruckus at that time of the morning that many of the residents jumped up and turned on their lights. That was like watching color television. I am sure that I saw one guy wearing a Mickey Mouse night gown.

From there I was back on Pacific Coast Hwy headed east to the Harbor Free Way to Long Beach. I got to Long Beach so quick. As soon as I spotted my dozers and earth-movers I backed in quickly. Throwing my gears into neutral, I instantly pulled my parking brake and engaged the PTO (power take off) as I jumped from the cab unreeling the diesel hose and climbing on the equipment while the truck was still rocking. Most of the time I was able to pump in excess of 55 gallons before the truck finished rocking. I would sometimes laugh and say, "Man, I am fast."

Driving for an oil company added color to the industry. Whenever a black person saw a black man in the truck I would always get a second take and up goes the Black Power sign. In the 1960's it was unheard of a black man to drive an oil company's truck. I suppose it was just as astonishing to the police, especially since I hadn't been issued uniforms yet.

"What are you doing driving this oil company's truck? I was asked.

"Making deliveries."

"Show me something with the company's name on it." I then pointed to the decal on the truck.

"No, no", he says, "Show me something in your wallet."

I gave him the dispatcher's business card with his phone numbers. He then let me go.

I discovered Balboa Beach while making a delivery to the Marina. It captured my interest over-whelmingly. There were attractive store front shopping areas on the west shore of the beach and for a fee the ferry took you and your car across the beach to shop and dine on the east shore. That in itself was impressive, especially to a first time guest. Balboa proved to be a haven of peace and tranquility.

It now appeared that everything was going right for me. When Hank arrived to the office at 7:00 a.m. he didn't have enough time to relax because I am in the driver's room waiting for another load. I was so nimble Hank didn't have enough work to keep me busy. Hank had Jimenez training a white boy on my previous route. I observed that on their first day out, they were back very early. I was surprised but thought the contractor had less equipment to fuel at the airport. What do you know; the next day everything hit the fan. The contractor was calling and screaming because his equipment was out of fuel. Now there's an emergency. Hank wanted the pussycat to pull him out of a hole. I really didn't mind at all. Hank was forced to see that I was doing a fantastic job all alone. When Dick came back from his vacation he said to me that as far as he is concerned I had done a heck of a job and he had promoted me to the ranks of a permanent truck driver. I really felt good about myself. I formulated slogans to keep me upbeat such as, 'No matter how hard you try you can't stop me now.'

I continued to dominate in the local delivery arena but not without an incident. I shared my truck with a Mexican guy who worked the night shift, most of us called him Fig. I used the truck from 5:00 a.m. to 2:00 p.m. Fig's hours were from 3:00 pm to12:00 pm. He was a lot larger than me and was full of dirty tricks. Let's just say, Fig was big and funky. Leaving the truck on flats three times a week was as common as breathing with him. Before I could load my truck I had to go across the street and change the tires. The thing that made the job so hard was the weight of the lug gun which was about seventy- five pounds. It was cold blooded for a guy to intentionally leave a fellow driver in that situation. The proper recourse was to confront the dispatcher because it certainly affects the product distribution. I tried to handle this situation in a peaceable manner, by letting

Dick know my deliveries were being delayed by changing Fig's flats before beginning my route.

I was never told whether Mr. Tyree confronted Fig or not, however when talking to one of Fig's friends I was told that he let him know he should be ashamed of himself. Of course Fig blew it off with a big laugh. I had no doubt in my mind that Fig had absolutely no concern for his fellow drivers. Therefore I said to myself, two can play this game. I knew the past would become present again and, keeping in mind the size and weight difference, whatever tactic I employed must be an act of silent retribution. Besides that, I have always believed; fun is in the planning.

Sad to say, less than two weeks later Fig was up to his old dirty tricks again. The mind is such an incredible feature of the human body. Many mornings I awoke from my sleep and knew it was going to be a funky day at work. So was the day when Fig attempted to pull another fast-one on me. I slowly approached my truck saying out loud, "I hope he didn't. I hope he didn't." Of course, I knew he did. He not only left me on one flat, but two.

"That's it." Was my verbal reply although no one other than me was there to hear what was said. I immediately began to enact my silent rage not by replacing the flat tires but by pumping air into the flat tires. Every fifteen minutes I systematically pulled over to check the tires. Surprising as it was, they were all up and holding. I was very happy about that because blow-outs, for the most part, are due to low air pressure and the dispatcher would most definitely chew my behind out about that. Even though both tires had a slow leak I only pumped air three times the whole day.

At the end of the shift all tires were still up. Since I was successful in not changing the flats, now it was time to teach Fig a little lesson. There was no doubt that he knew the condition he left the truck in, therefore it was time for justice. I made it quite obvious that he was busted by draining all the air out of the inside dual, and reduced the outside dual to less than one half of the required amounts. Guest what?

The next day all tires on the truck were as they should have been. Fig and I never see each other during shift change but this day unlike any other day he and I came face to face. As I headed for the parking lot here comes Fig walking toward me looking like Bluto. Trying to keep a straight face as we approached each other I go, "how is it going Fig?"

"What's happenin' pussycat?"

I said "everything's cool."

Both of us kept walking in the opposite direction. When I got into my car I couldn't help but crack up. From that day forward I had no further problem with Fig. Like my dad always said, *don't be nobody's fool.*

CHAPTER SIX

I LEARNED ALL THAT I needed to know about the contractor's truck and I was more than pleased with my skills. The word had got around the terminal that I was the dispatcher's 'go-to guy'. Dick Tyree was anxious to put me on the barrel truck working directly for him. But since the rotation was to be according to seniority I had to wait my turn.

Right about now I am just about as happy as a mosquito in a nudist camp. It is about midweek and what do you know, the phone rings and it's Numero Uno, the head doctor, the star of the team.

He tells me that there's going to be a party this weekend in Altadena at this bad pad in a cul-de-sac overlooking the Rose Bowl. "Be there or be square, he says."

Saturday rolled around and I was there, but late as usual. Most of the Doctors were there, but The Head Doctor came solo. As I walked up a beautiful Black girl answered the door. She introduced herself as Tracy Jones a co-host of the party, and took my coat as she smiled radiantly. The girl didn't even know what she had. She had a beautiful smile, a pleasing personality and a gorgeous shape, there were no defects. She's a pearl of a girl. She was the type of girl white folks didn't mind hugging. Even though there was an attraction on both of our part, I spent most of the evening dancing with the little young girl in the white jump suit, doing the worm, who was emitting more signals than a Boeing Jet.

As I was about to leave Tracy made darn sure she was the one who brought me my coat. I must say that both of us picked upon each other's telepathy. My greatest concern at the time was if she was seeing someone. I asked the fellas and they didn't know. I thought to myself, a girl that fine had to be talking to someone. Time passed but I never could get her off my mind. Perhaps we would meet again somehow.

Meanwhile, back at the job, I got a break. Dick Tyree put this big 250 pound white boy on the barrel truck. His first day out of training, he only made five deliveries out of thirteen orders. He told Dick he just couldn't do the Pasadena route, it was too hard. The Company gave him another job working in the office. Now, the ball bounced my way once again. I was asked if I was ready for the barrel truck. "Oh sure", was my reply. In fact I was thrilled about that because I thought maybe by coincidence I would see Tracy, with her fine self.

Dick gave me a trainer. He was Fig's friend Chuck

"Katt, you think you can handle these heavy behind barrels?"

My reply was a resounding, "Oh yeah".

When we pulled up to the first stop Chuck says, "Let me show you how it's done." Chuck brought down the first order on the tailgate. He showed me where the customer wanted the product. He then began to roll the first barrel to the spot and release it.

"You think you got it?" "Yeah, I got it."

"Take the next one over there then."

I managed to roll it about three feet and stumbled, about to fall. Chuck catches the barrel holding it until I got my balance.

He says, "Look Katt, you have to handle these barrels like you are dancing with a big fat woman."

I could relate to that somewhat, so I caught on pretty quick. During my two weeks of training I never saw Tracy even though I hoped I would.

Chuck cut me a loose after two weeks and I was on my own once again. Driving the barrel truck was exciting. I met a lot more people and the job was more versatile. I learned early in the game that vehicle accidents would get you fired. One thing I can say about those little young crazy white boys in their middle twenties, they had good taste. They weren't out running into Mustangs and Pinto's, no they were up in Hollywood and Beverly Hills crashing into and backing over Mercedes and Jaguars. If they were at fault, nine times out of ten they were fired. I asked one of the dispatchers about Porky because I hadn't seen him lately.

"Is he on vacation?

"Yeah," said the dispatcher. "He's on a long one. He won't be coming back."

After so many white boys got fired, the company hired quite a few blacks. Now the words, 'reverse discrimination' were being echoed.

I suppose some guys are just accident prone. On this particular day one of the guys was driving the harbor Free-way, in the downtown area, when the traffic stopped abruptly. A car ran into the rear of one of our four-thousand gallon tankers. The door flew open and the driver fell out of the truck onto the free-way, a consequence of not wearing his seat belt. Since the truck was minus its driver, it rolled into a ditch. The guy was a little bit older and had been with the company for some time. Fortunately, he was not fired and through observation the Katt became instinctively wise. I could almost smell an accident before it happened and would not go anywhere near one because I could be stuck in traffic for hours. If things began to look downright funky to me I would exit the free-way and get back on some time later.

Delivering barrels of oil was much more physical than pumping diesel fuel; therefore, I decided to do a little barbering every other weekend when the fellas came in.

Working for a large company was neat because it had wealthy clients, such as, Universal Studios, Burbank Studios, Paramount Pictures and other conglomerates. We delivered to all municipalities in every town in southern California. The customers and their workers were simply amazed at the way I handled the big oil drums. I had those barrels spinning like a top, and with a flip of the wrist within six feet I had the barrels spinning on its rim and stopping exactly where the customer wanted them. When I knew I had an audience I would really put on a show.

The fun part with the barrel truck was when I was able to sneak around the studios and see the difference scenes everyone else sees at the movies. Inside the compound of the movie industry was a gas station and that is always the main point of the delivery. While I was there some of the attractions I saw were 'the collapsing bridge' and 'Jaws'.

I was also amazed to see the Eldorado convertible driven in one of the Dirty Harry movies. I just had to stop my truck and take a closer look at the interior which was a clean leopard skin and the grill was of gold chrome with a figurine of a little man holding a stick of lit dynamite in his hand, and inscribed below it was the name "Willie Dynamite", that was fascinating.

A year had passed since I last saw Tracy. I got an invitation threw mail from her inviting me to a party at her house. In fact I received two invitations. One was sent to Aunt E's house and the other to my sister's place. I learned later that she sent invitations to everyone she thought might know me. I readily responded to the invite.

After arriving there and getting reacquainted I realized that I had been driving right pass her house many times on my way to Jet Propulsion Laboratories in Pasadena. We danced together most of the evening. I wore a grey hound tooth, checkered suit which was tailored, but the girl had sized me up the first night we meet. I had to know if she was seeing anyone and she told me no, not really. I found out there was a guy talking to her, and I was told that he loved the ground she walked on. In fact he still does. After we commenced talking she started throwing rocks at him.

Tracy introduced me to her family that night. They all seemed to be very nice, including her grandfather, but he thought I was just a little too cool. I told her family my name was Melvin Rea. Tracy introduced me as Melvin and could say it so sweet. She had a brother named Melvin; of course he said the girls called him 'Sweet Black'. After being married for some time he changed his name to Mr. Melody.

It was a pleasure being in Tracy's presence once again, but as soon as some of the other dudes found out I was seeing Tracy, here they came knocking on her door, trying to skin the Katt. They saw my Cadillac parked at the curb, white on white, in white. I heard her tell one of them with the big mustache that he wasn't being respectful because he came over unannounced and she had company. She sent him on his way.

I honestly believe those guys admired me, but they just couldn't stand me. It seemed as if Tracy and I couldn't stay away from each other. Some called 'it sugar pie honey bunch'. In fact, we basked in each other's radiance. We became close, closer than a ham on a country hog, closer than a collar on a dog. After being with Tracy for some time I realized that my weekends were getting away from me, so I could no longer answer the bell at the barber shop. It was a T.K.O. (technical knockout) I am now devoting my weekends and holidays to Tracy. In reality, I hated to leave my homeboys hanging, but my love and devotion went to Tracy.

Tracy and I dated consistently for a year, then we took our vows as husband and wife and, of course, the head doctor was in the wedding. I remained in West LA and sometime later we became the managers of a twenty unit apartment complex.

After being with the oil company for seven years Tracy and I are doing just great and trucking had become second nature. I wasn't bored, but I was too good at what I did. I was determined to make my job a little more exciting. On my way back from deliveries I would practice driving down the Harbor Free-way with my eyes closed and counting to twenty-five before I opened them again. To be truthful, I was good at it. This little exhibition was only the beginning, I think the most shocking display of talent was when I locked the throttle in at 55 miles per hour and steered the truck with my feet as I held my hands up in the air. I got commuters attention by blowing the air horn. One passenger in lane two touched the driver and said, "Just look at that fool."

After re-entering the terminal, the first assignment was to kick off the empty barrels onto the dock. It is noteworthy that at the very end of the dock there were railroad tracts. You see the company had its own spur. This is where Union Pacific dropped off tank cars of special product such as gear lube and antifreeze. The tank cars were left on the tracts for Blu to off load by pumping the products into the storage tanks.

When leaving the dock we had to drive around the back of the terminal to the front side to park the trucks. Things proved to be just a little too easy for me. I always left the dock with my stick shift in second low. Once I turned the corner and straightened my truck parallel with the building I then hopped out of the truck and trotted along beside it with the door open. I am sure I did this for months. I want you to know, that this day unlike all other days something strange happened. I kicked off my empties as always and got into my little creative routine. I noticed the truck was rolling faster than I expected. In fact it was getting away from me. I had to run faster than I ever had to catch up with the truck. I had to really shake my set of doubles.

When I did catch up with it I hopped inside the cab and stopped it. I sat in the cab huffing and puffing for about five minutes. Between the huffs and puffs I said out loud, "I almost tore up these white folks truck." I come to realize that I had left the truck in second overdrive instead of second low. I then wondered to myself what kind of lie I would have told if that truck had got away from me. I decided right then that I would never do any crap like that again.

I never told Tracy about my little episodes. I dodged a bullet so it's best to let things stay as they were. I think the thing that frustrated me most was trying to make deliveries during lunch hour when the little old rich ladies were out cruising on the freeway, especially the Hollywood Freeway. They were in their Rolls-Royces and Mercedes, dressed to kill, and would not speed up or move over for anything. After trying to persuade them to get out of the my way and since it did not work then I waited until I approached an under-pass and turned off the ignition for a few seconds and turned it back on, it generated a sound as if a miniature bomb had gone off. Of course, that got their attention; nevertheless, I came to the conclusion that it might not be a nice thing to do, so I no longer used those kinds of tactics.

No matter what tactics or skill I employed, I seemed to always have to pay the consequences for my actions. One of my exhibitions on the free-way cost me a day in court. Not to be disingenuous, all California freeways are controlled by the Highway Patrol. We refer to them as free-way cruisers. Officer Sly wasn't impressed with my steering the truck with my feet; consequently I was cited for reckless driving. Nonetheless, in my opinion there was nothing reckless about my driving at all; pure raw skills would have been a better description of my performance. There is one thing I am sure of, I didn't want that citation to appear on my driving record; so I elected to take a chance in traffic court. That particular day Judge Marylyn Lynch was presiding. She began by checking the docket to see if the officers and defendants were present. If the officer did not appear then the case was dismissed, but unfortunately, not so in my case.

While waiting for my name to be called, I was quite impressed with the young black man Joshua Johnson, who alleged that officer Ketchum and his partner had stopped him a number of times just to poke fun at him. Of course, officer Ketchum said Mr. Johnson was speeding. Quiet as it is kept, the officers always sound dignified and exact in a court of law. Mr. Johnson took the stand and pleaded not guilty. He asked the officer to state his name for the record and he then turns to the Judge, "Your Honor, I am a law student at UCLA and I have an old raggedy car that I drive to school in every day, officer Ketchum and his partner know my car by sight, and here they come. They know I am trying to get to school, but they just have to pull me over and harass me."

"This day in question Mr. Johnson, was on a Saturday," says the Judge, "tell me about that".

"It was early in the morning your Honor. I was on my way to my grandmother's house and here they come again."

"Officer Ketchum said you were speeding", interjected the Judge.

"Your Honor, I wasn't speeding, that's just another way of harassing me."

Judge Lynch asked the officer, "What was the danger in Mr. Johnson driving at that rate of speed".

He responded by saying, "there were children on the street at that time".

"How many", asked the Judge?

"About five or six" was his reply.

Mr. Johnson objected by saying, "Your Honor, that's not true at all, 7:00 o clock on Saturday morning kids are at home watching pussycat and tweedy bird."

The entire court cracked up. Judge Lynch told the officer she was going to dismiss him at that time and notify Mr. Johnson of her decision through mail.

I was impressed with the young man's defense; nevertheless looking and listening to him it was easy to discern he was from South Central and left a large window of opportunity open for me. At least, I thought so. Now it's my turn. Judge Lynch asked me and Officer Sly to take the stand and asked me how did I plea? "Not guilty your Honor". Officer Sly proceeded to tell the court that I was driving reckless by steering the truck with my feet.

"Mister Katt do you have any questions for the Officer" asked the Judge?

"Yes I do your Honor; first of all I would like to say good morning to your Honor, the officer and the people of this court.

"Officer Sly", I asked, "what lane did the so called reckless driving occur"?

"Lane four", he says.

"Okay, lane four, correct?"

"Yes"

"Where were my hands?"

"Above your shoulders", he contended.

"Was there anyone in the vehicle other than me"?

His answer was "no".

"Okay, if that was the case, who would you say controlled the accelerator?"

"I don't know" was his reply.

"Officer Sly, perhaps you would like to demonstrate to the court how I was able to steer the truck with my feet with my hands above my shoulders and control the accelerator at the same time."

"No", was what he said.

"No?" The court was silent.

"Your Honor, I would like to appeal to your intelligence. Officer Sly stated that all of this happened in lane four; if I had been operating the vehicle in a reckless manner I surely would have drifted into other lanes and he would have said so. This thing about me driving with my feet is unheard of. Cheep cars and commercial vehicles don't have cruise control. Your Honor, a black man driving this type of truck for an oil company is a new phenomenon (as I gradually slid my fingers down my cheeks) many people, simply are not ready for the change.

"Mister Katt, do you have any further questions?"

"No I don't Your Honor, I rest my case."

"Officer Sly, I am going to dismiss you at this time, and mister Katt I will notify you of my decision through mail".

Every case heard that morning from A through J, Judge Lynch made her decision from the bench, with the exception of Joshua Johnson and Melvin Rea Katt.

I thought I had put up a great defense, but oddly enough two weeks later I received a letter from Judge Lynch conveying her decision, "guilty as charged."

Of course I was disappointed, but it was quite educational.

It looks like I am about to face another challenge. Here it is in mid-summer, it is extremely hot and muggy in the valley. The Valley I have reference to is as follows: San Fernando, Pacoima, Northridge, Topanga-Canyon, Agoura, and Calabasas. Of course I do not want to omit Semi Valley. These are some of the hottest towns on the northern side of Southern California. So what's the problem? It is the largest and longest route by far. To make matters worse most of the white boys didn't want to work that route in the summer time.

If a driver doesn't reach the downtown area by three o'clock in the afternoon his goose is cooked. I was asked by Dick Tyree if I would take the valley route. Of course I said yes. The senior guys thought it was a real bad deal for a relatively new driver. I will probably have to do more work than the white guys anyway, so let the good times roll. I weighed in at 163 pounds and brown all year round. The heat probably wouldn't hurt me at all; at least I thought it wouldn't.

I was assigned a larger truck and had more orders to deliver. I didn't have a trainer because it was assumed that all I needed was a map book. The first day I wasn't able to complete the route and did not make it back in before everyone had gone home. I came in early the next day and had to listen to the other guy's harassment.

"Hey, puss, puss, pussycat", stuttered Tommy Lee.

"I thought we-we weeee was gonna have to sen-sen send a search, search party out fur yo-yo Lil - tail". Of course all the guys laughed, but I didn't say a word.

One of the assistant dispatchers felt sad for me. He asked," Do you think you will be able to do the route?"

I responded by saying, "oh yeah, I am going to whip it."

Each day I got better and better. Whipping it I did, but really we whipped and beat up each other. When I got my orders for the next day's run I always asked the senior drivers how to get to the next stop. It was indeed a tough route. I was out there thinking and stinking. My shirt was soaking wet with sweat. My fingernails grew some of the fastest and my hair grew some of the longest. My ears got so hairy they could have easily been mistaken for something else, so I was told with a bit of exaggeration. I had to take a pair of my Oster clippers and give my under arms a crew-cut. Believe it or not I did get a tan. Lee took me to the side and told me I had to take time out and cut some of that crap off my head. To this very day he claims he doesn't remember.

After a couple of months my mission had been thoroughly accomplished. I had become so good at what I did; I could make all my deliveries in a tuxedo and never get it dirty. I even had the distinct privilege of training other drivers, but failed drastically in one area, nonetheless. Frank was a fine worker and loved by our customers. I just could not teach him how to keep his uniform clean while making deliveries, to save my life. When he returned to the terminal, he looked like he had been wallowing in a pig pen.

Dick Tyree was ready for me to move on to other things. I had acquired seniority with the company and had three weeks of vacation with pay. Tracy and I decided to take a two week vacation to visit my parents. Dad had aged some, yet he still looked good. All he talked about was him being ready to retire and raising his cows. In fact, in a little less than three years from that date Dad did retire.

I returned to work with a new assignment delivering gasoline to older and small volume gas stations which was relatively easy, no heat, no sweat. I always believed, with a four inch hose it's a splash. Nevertheless, there was one thing weird about the older stations, they had outside rest rooms and the vent pipes stood high above the toilets. One of the stations downtown on Olympic Blvd. was a task to get into, but it was manageable.

After backing in, I proceed to drop my load. Evidently the guy inside the restroom decided to smoke a cigarette and suddenly the roof blew off. I immediately shut off the gas flow and the flame went out. I must say, that was the hottest crap that guy ever took. When I got in all the drivers were there waiting for me. As I walked into the drivers room one of the guys threw me a roll of toilet tissue.

"What is this for?" I asked.

"It is Just in case you forgot to wipe your tail."

I had out grown everything I had tried, therefore I made it known I wanted to try out the eighteen wheeler delivering a forty-five foot trailer of product to marketing stations. The fifteen foot truck was a Kenworth with a thirteen speed road ranger. I was told there wasn't an opening, but I could train to be a relief driver. I was trained and certified to perform this task when called on.

This was a cool job because we went to a different city everyday and the pay was considerably more. We went to Bakersfield and Saint Louis Obispo to the north. We had Victorville and Barstow to the east and some smaller towns in between. Las Vegas was our north- eastern boundary. San Diego and El Centro was the southeast drop off point.

It didn't matter what kind of work I went into someone was always sitting around waiting for a joke. One day Tommy's wife saw me driving the semi-truck and told him, that the Katt looks like a little fly in that big old truck.

While sitting in the driver's room one day Tommy leans over and touched me. He says, "Hey Katt, my-my, kids saw, saw you go, go, going across the par, par, parking lot the other day, an, and one of them said, "The Katt sho-sho, thanks he, he's cool don't he daddy?"

I asked him what he said. "I said he sure does baby." It didn't take very long to find out what the guys really thought of the Katt.

It appeared though, that I was at the end of the line, and there was no room for further advancement. I had ten years with the company and for the most part, still had a creative mind. I convinced myself there must be life after trucking. Tracy and I had one child and decided to purchase a home and move from Los Angeles to another town in LA County. We were ready for a change and I had already driven my Cadillac through one energy crisis between 1974 and 1975 while others were running on empty. Buying a home shouldn't be much of a problem at all. During the early and mid 1970's the company was deeply concerned about their image. Many in the public sector believed the energy crisis was artificially created by the oil companies, government, and the Arabs. They pointed their fingers directly to them for skyrocketing oil prices and sitting in long lines at gas stations. This brought widespread panic to the nation. The Watergate scandal in the early 1970's exacerbated things.

Many sources emphasized that the actual "crisis" in the United States stemmed from our own domestic political and social circumstances than any single event that might have occurred overseas. Fuel allocation was such a dilemma. I sat in the driver's room many days waiting for the okay to deliver a load. Some gas stations were forced to shut down because of fuel shortages. Gas gulping cars became undesirable, and many Americans turned to buying smaller European and Japanese cars.

The 1970's gradually came to an end and we were able to keep on trucking, but the question that popped into my mind was how long I would be able to continue. I began to really appreciate my oldest brother Ernie and his wife Gloria. They had always been supportive of the family. Both Ernie and his wife are strong advocates for education. Ernie put himself through school and served as a probation official with the Los Angeles County Department of Corrections for many years.

Both of them later became educators with the LA County School District. Ernie encouraged me to continue my education and he would ask me questions such as: "What is the mortality rate for a truck driver?" I didn't quite know at the time, but I did know that the chances were much greater for me getting hurt as a truck driver than him falling off his chair and sticking a pencil up his behind.

Even though I was fully vested with the company and my seniority was gaining momentum, marvelous as it may seem, something was still missing, (In other words) I still didn't know what I wanted to be when I grew up. Deep within I desired to be in a profession that required a little more sophistication. I was not in the least crazy about sales, but loved the challenge of acquisition.

In the early 1980's California real estate was going strong. I went to Real Estate school at night and drove the truck by day. I studied real estate for six months using the cab of my Peter Built truck as a library and workshop. I took the examination for the Real Estate license and flunked it the first time. My greatest dilemma was my inability to finish the exam in the allotted time. I was not clerical at all, in order to pass state exams I definitely had to pick up the paste.

The lack of speed was my worst enemy. I took the exam for the second time and I can tell you unequivocally that the second exam is always harder than the first. I kid you not; school was out, I passed the exam. I started a part time job with a privately owned real estate company (dba) West End Realty.

I tell you, real estate was exciting, for a number of reasons. Pay was good and I met lots of people. I was able to dazzle expressions like, "make me an offer." I sold many homes to first time buyers who had families and wanted to get out of the war zone. In the city, it seemed like dudes were breaking into homes and cars for recreation. Some dudes were so cold; they broke into John the Baptist's Volkswagen, stole his seats, and then left him a milk crate near the steering wheel where the seat used to be.

The homes in the suburbs of LA were slightly above the median family dwellings and the rush was on. I always asked for a referral and told the person I would make it worth his efforts. Commission was really great for only a few hours of work. My broker handled all escrows since I was trucking full time.

I had tons of fun working real estate for two years when I get a call from Mom stating that dad had a stroke and was in the Hospital. After being there for a week Dad developed pneumonia and was in ICU not expected to live. Although I heard the prognosis, it did not fully register, after all, other people die, but not my Dad. Surely Dr. Smith is mistaken. My Dad is a hell raiser and a fornicator; he had gone through the Great Depression and survived segregation. My Dad could jump six feet and talk all day. Just two weeks ago I was told he was running around flirting with Sally Mae.

"I asked Dr. Smith, are we talking about the same black man, Thom Ira Katt that was in room 113?" I had a little problem with the reality of Dad dying. Nevertheless, two days later, he breezed right out of our lives. It seemed so unfair for dad to have worked all this time to retire and less than two years from that time he dies. I thought for sure he would last for another ten years. Of course, I remember Mom's quote from the ninetieth Psalms verse 10 "In themselves the days of our years are seventy years; and if because of special mightiness they are eighty years, yet their insistence is on trouble and hurtful things; for it must quickly pass by, and away we fly."

With Dad passing away we entered into a brand new episode of our lives. There is Tracy and me and three kids. Mom was all alone with several acres of land, about fifty heads of cows and calves, a tractor and equipment she could not work. What would Mom do since Dad is no longer around? I am much too young to retire and was not in a position to quit my job and move back, even though it was always in my mind to go back someday and beautify the place.

If a guy didn't have ample income, the people in that part of the South probably would not give him a break. I soon received the news that two of Mom's grandchildren were going to live with her. That was good news. What was even better was the fact that Mom's nephew we all called TC was moving to Texas with the intent of taking over the heir property. He promised to buy twenty heads of cattle from Mom, the tractor and equipment as well.

TC encouraged me to buy a few cows from Mom and get started. He felt that within a few years I would be ready to move back and I would already have my start. I ran that by Mom and she was okay with the plan. I bought three cows from her and she gave me one more. TC volunteered to take care of my cows and Mom's as long as I gave him a hand when I came to visit. He and I had a beautiful relationship, we were just like brothers, and we worked well together. I was somewhat relieved the way things worked out because this bought me a little more time. Not long after TC moved back one of my sisters and her husband moved near Mom. I no longer worried about Mom because there was enough family to take care of her.

Everything is going well with me at work. I have added another five years to my seniority, but we are now in the mid 1980's and a recession has set in. People were losing their homes, primarily because of layoffs. Foreclosures were definitely on the rise. For sale signs were growing out of the ground like wild flowers.

Home owners were literally drowning in mortgage debt. The Nation had got caught up in a psychological frenzy. Interest rates were going through the roof and the buyers could be conservative because they had many homes to choose from. In the LA Times every Sunday near the Foreclosure section, a well known guy would advertise his class on foreclosures for $299. After watching his ad for six months I noticed that he was running a special for $99 and I decided to jump on it. I had come to a conclusion that when a man had made all the money he could make in a business he would write a book or teach classes to enhance his riches.

What I learned about foreclosures was amazing. The most difficult job was getting a home owner to talk to you. A person whose home is being foreclosed does not want to talk about selling his home, it's too painful. He wants to save it at all cost. In the class I learned how to get the owner to call me. There is one thing you need to understand about an owner in foreclosure. You can mail him $100 checks all day long and they would never get cashed. He will not open your letter. After working this business for two weeks I called the guy up and asked him what should be my response rate. He told me a good response rate would be three to five persons out of every twenty letters I send out. Well, I'm getting eight to twelve out of every twenty. He told me that was excellent. I suppose I learned a lot more than he expected. To be quite frank about it, I got a lot of people out of foreclosure and made me and the broker money. I sometimes wonder what's with these men I meet. The first foreclosure I worked on was with a husband and wife. I had everything worked out for them. I called back a few days later to see how things were going and the wife told me her husband had gotten another guy to help them, but she would rather work with me. I told her okay, and I hope things go well for them. She called me back a few days later and told me they were going to do business with me, because she didn't like that guy in the first place.

I am happy to say; sometimes the women are a better judge of character. I designed myself another business card with a catchy slogan that said, "I arrange fast loans and freeze foreclosures, Melvin Rea Katt (AKA) Doctor Freeze. When the home owners call they always ask, "What do you mean, you freeze foreclosures?" My classic answer was, "I will arrange you a fast loan and freeze the action of the foreclosure."

As time passed by, I began considering ways of leave the oil company and becoming financially free. Nevertheless, there were so many ups and downs in the economy I felt it was better to become financially free first and then leave. After all, it was trucking that took me to the dance, cha, cha, cha. Although I felt I would be successful in anything I touched, I wasn't in any way comfortable in putting all my trust in a stranger. As I was in this mode of thinking a friend of ours gave Tracy and I a visit.

He offered us an opportunity to become financially independent working part time. Tracy had become a legal secretary making good money, but extra money is always appealing to a Californian. He explained that the business he was in was a multi-trillion dollar business and we could become a part of it just by working part time. Tracy wanted to know what kind of business he was a part of. "I'm glad you asked." He said. "It is a financial service business."

He went on to state that he and his associates have insurance licenses. Tracy responded quickly by saying, "I don't want to sell any insurance."

"Wait just a minute," He says, "You don't have to sale anything. Just give me the names of three of your friends and I will talk to them for you. Now here is the good part, for everyone that does business with me, you will get 40% of the business volume; of course you will need an insurance license. I want you to know that's not a problem. I will send you to school for just one day and I guarantee you will pass the test. Here is another thing; Melvin Rea has a real estate license and people buying homes need insurance. You guys have an inside tract, you might as well make some of this money. There is something I didn't mention, some of the people I speak to will want to get into the business also, and they will become your people."

I responded by saying, "You know it does sound pretty good, but I have a little too much going on at the time. I don't have a problem with Tracy doing the business. In fact, I will help her."

Sure enough, just as Freddy Joe said, Tracy passed the exam with no problem. That guy was incredible, everyone he talked to did business with Tracy, and it was amazing that 20% of those people wanted to get into the business. He was as slick as Vaseline on a door knob.

With Freddy's and my little help before long Tracy had built quite a promising organization. Of course I kept my mind focused on Texas. I had been with the oil company long enough to get four weeks of vacation. I used two weeks with Tracy and the kids and twice a year I spent four to five days in Texas beautifying the place. When the boys were on break from school they went with me. I spent thousands and thousands of dollars on dozer work and believe it or not, it wasn't long before the entire property was transformed. Many times people came and said it was the prettiest property on the road. My mother at ninety-one years old still says, "I sure wish Kitt could see this now. He always wanted it to look like this, but wasn't able to do it." Through all of it Tracy was congenial as all get out. The thing I regret the most to this day, is when I arrived in Texas I went to work right away and would not call her until later on in the evening. That was an error.

Even though my heart was in Texas, I had my eye on Tracy's business as well. Freddy met with Tracy and me one Sunday evening over dinner. He tells me that Tracy's organization is growing so fast he couldn't keep up. He made it known that he needed help. It was recommended that I get my insurance license and assist Tracy with her fantastic business and since the business was booming I might as well have a legal share in it, I thought.

I went to the Steve Lewis School of Learning for only one Saturday and took the test and passed it. I was proud of the results because this was one state exam I didn't have to take for the second time. I was placed in the organization directly beneath Tracy. I stood in front of the mirror in the bathroom, which was my favorite position, and said, "Now I have a master barber's license, a real estate license, and on top of that, I have an insurance license. That's not too shabby for a little country boy." Both Tracy and I applied and received non-resident insurance licenses for the State of Texas. I have to admit, I had to chuckle just a bit when remembering Freddy Joe's favorite expression, "You got to pay for your education."

In view of it all, my stability, as I see it, was still in trucking. Undoubtedly, some big wheel from the downtown cooperate office, came up with a bright idea and a great incentive.

The company's first annual truck roadeo was born. This was quite unique because it was designed with the safe drivers in mind and I had many years of safe driving. To qualify as a participant in the contest the driver cannot have a chargeable accident within the past year. The first annual safe driving roadeo was set up at Dodger Stadium in Los Angeles. To begin with, there was a safety inspection of the type of truck each participant drove. He must find all defective items on the truck. For each defective item that was not reported five points was deducted from his score.

All drivers began with a score of 100. The next challenge was the obstacle course. We had to back our truck into a blind alley and stop six inches before hitting the wall. If the wall was hit, twenty five points were deducted. Each inch away from the mark, one point was deducted. They set up a barricade with a ninety degree angle, then working safely through the serpentine without touching the cones and out to a forty- five degree angle, then to the last right angle and down the diminishing alley without hitting anything.

In my first safe driving contest I competed with Tommy Lee for First place. Nevertheless I came in with the Second place trophy. The company also set up a safe driving course for the truck driver's wives with a little Luv pickup truck. Tracy won the First place trophy in that contest. Of course the guys said the company should hire Tracy to drive for them instead of me. That Saturday night after the roadeo we all went to dinner at one of the finest places in LA. This was all arranged and paid for by the company. After dinner the supervisors talked about how things went that day. Tommy bragged that I could never beat him.

The second annual roadeo, I not only beat him, I retired him. He no longer had the courage to participate in the competition again.

The competition was particularly tough for the wives because all of us were friends and each of the wives wanted their husband to win. There were other incentives to having a good score. The driver who had the overall highest score received $500.00 in gift products. The truck roadeo was only held two consecutive years at Dodger Stadium. The next year the company flew all drivers and their wives to Northern California. After the company initiated the change from Dodger stadium to other locations things became more interesting. San Diego was definitely a treat and Las Vegas wasn't too shabby either.

This family event grew so remarkably big that friends and family came from near and far to join in the festivities. There was no slack of hands when it came to food stuff. We had plenty of barbeque, corn on the cob, baked beans and rice, hamburgers, hot dogs, hot links and any kind of desert our hearts desired. There were drinks to no end. There were kiddy rides, toys, balloons, popcorn, peanuts, snow cones and cotton candy. The company even provided milk for the babies, in event the mothers weren't producing.

The roadeo was such a success that the company decided to have a three foot trophy with the names of the division winners engraved on it. This trophy would remain in the winning division for at least one year or until another division won. There were six divisions, the Southern, Northern, Mid-west, Alaska, Oregon and Nevada. If my memory serves me right, the trophy never left our division.

No one seemed to mind at all having four days off from work with pay and being put up in a nice motel with all you could eat. Safe driving was a way of life with me; the little perks were only a natural by-product. My first year of safe driving I received a bronze buckle and the following four years the company had rubies placed into the buckle. The sixth year I received a silver buckle. The next four years they had emeralds set in place. The beginning of my eleventh anniversary the company presented me with a gold buckle. Diamonds inserted for the following four years gave the buckle a touch of elegance. Make no mistake; the gold buckle is still super sharp to this very day.

Five days have already passed by and the annual truck roadeo is over. All drivers returned to their respective assignments as the hype wore off. I had to be somewhat ambidextrous and keep my mouth closed at work when it came to things I was doing while off duty. Tracy's business was above the run way and flying high. Our investment strategy was: Buy Term and Invest the Difference.

Consequently, we needed a securities license to complete the job. Freddy Joe had a securities license, but he was already strung out. To better serve our clients and the organization, someone in the immediate rank needed to step up. I had no doubt in my mind it had to be Tracy or myself. To invest our clients in mutual funds and variable annuities the agent must have a securities license. Since Tracy was the leader of the group, it would be most appropriate for her to assume leadership. But I must inform you, the securities license is no fly by night acquisition.

Tracy went to the Steve Lewis School of learning for two weekends and later took the examination which was done on the computer. She failed the exam and expressed her lack of desire to take it again. First of all, she felt it was a little too much, her being a mother, wife, employee, and at the same time operating a business. I responded by saying, "have no fear, Melvin Rea is here."

The thing she feared the most, was me being computer illiterate. Respectfully, she goes on to say, "Baby, that test is tough. Series Six exam is three hours long and Series Sixty-three is one and a half hours and that is a lot of testing, especially if you are not familiar with the computer." "Oh, I'll just have to learn, won't I?"

I have now assumed my familiar position, studying in the cab of the truck and listening to investment terminology as I drove along. It was fun expanding my horizon in an area that required even more sophistication. I truly had to be professional and impressive for people to give me their hard earned money to invest for them I studied for six weeks and filed for an exam date.

After receiving the date I continued to study and went to Steve Lewis on weekends. On the day of the exam I drove to Newport Beach and took the test. Not unexpected, I flunked the exam. Arriving back home Tracy asked, "How did you do?"

I responded by saying, "I flunked."

"That test was sort of difficult, wasn't it?" asked Tracy.

"No, it wasn't really that difficult, I was just too jiving slow. Next time, school is out. It will be all over."

"You really think so? Tracy asked.

"Do I think so? I know so. Ain't nothing short about the Katt, not even his tail. The next time baby, I'm letting it all hang out."

She smiled and said, "Okay daddy."

Tracy owned a computer that would accept diskettes, and right away I used my credit card to order a securities test package which included five diskettes for exams, Series Six, as well as Series Sixty-three. Every available moment, I was on that computer testing for the big day. Whenever I scored eighty-five percent and above for three times that particular test would delete itself. I was disappointed with that little mechanism and I decided to call the software company to inform them that the diskette wasn't working. Upon receiving a new diskette I purposely did not score over eighty-four on any of the test after the first time so I could continue testing.

After studying in the cab of my truck and testing in the privacy of my home for five weeks I filed to retake the exam. Tracy wanted to know if I wanted to go back to Steve Lewis for a refresher course. My answer was no. In fact I told her, she might as well put that money in the cookie jar, because now, I am two times twice as fast.

When I received my test date I was foaming at the bit. I couldn't see anything but success on the horizon. On the exam the word problems were much more extensive, but it didn't matter, the bigger the band, the sweeter the music was my attitude. After a couple of hours of battling the beast I completed the exam before my time was up, and was afraid to go back for review. I had a funny feeling that I might erase some of my answers, since I wasn't that familiar with the computer. Therefore, I elected to press the 'End Exam' bottom. Guess what appeared on the screen? It read "Congratulations, you have successfully completed the Series Six Securities examination."

I was so thrilled and excited about passing the exam, now I can legally talk investments, write them and get paid for doing so. Tracy was really happy for me and could breathe a sigh of relief. Business was not as usual, I had just accomplished something that sixty-percent of the people usually fail. As a favor, I began to invest for people who were not in our immediate group. I taught all in our group that they were not without power, because they could place their clients in IRA's and single premium deferred annuities and get paid for it. I immediately filed for Series Sixty-Three exam, the Blue Sky Laws. Rules, Laws and Regulations were my forte, therefore I knocked that little test out with plenty of time to spare.

The curtain was still up for me because of my ambidextrous ability. Tracy's R.V.P (Regional Vice President) Hank Snow convinced us that her organization would grow much faster if Tracy allowed him to place me as head of her business, because people would rather follow a man than a woman. After speaking with Hank, we did so well, Hank presented me the M.V.P Award. He took that opportunity to go into a butt chewing frenzy, "I would rather have one man that is cocky and get the job done than a whole lot of people sitting around talking and doing nothing." Everyone looked at me and laughed. He also contended, "All you had was Melvin Rea Katt and a hand full of women."

Meanwhile, I am still trucking for the man and in case of an emergency who do they call? They call the Katt, because I was the Kitty with the real nitty gritty. Such energy landed me in the Hospital with a broken jaw. Obviously, it happened at a most inopportune time. My mouth was wired shut for six weeks and no one could visualize me with my mouth shut. Many times prior to my accident my friends would ask me, "Katt, why do you talk all the time?"

My answer was classic, "Well, I can't sing." I lost twenty-five pounds, and after going back to work one of the drivers called me Skinny Bone Jones. It took some time for me to fit back into the routine of things. I just didn't have the same energy, nor did I have the same vigor. I had time to reflect back on big brother's question posed earlier, "What is the mortality rate of a truck driver?"

CHAPTER SEVEN

FOR THE NEXT FIVE years I did everything possible to bounce back. I began taking Ginseng, the rejuvenator, all B-vitamins and a number of regenerative herbs, but nonetheless, that barrel truck was truly whipping the Katt's tail. Everyone knew it including me. I had no problem investing money for people on the side, because that within itself wasn't exhausting at all, but nevertheless handling those 500 pound barrels of product really had the Katt's tail dragging. My performances were showing a serious sign of a chill, even though I never thought of anything debilitating or potentially lethal, I got hit by something I never saw coming.

I had no idea how long I could continue this type of work. I was confident though, I could always go into the office and do several different jobs, but The Katt did not like being caged. I searched my mind with great veracity, being careful not to throw caution to the wind. If I left the oil company I would certainly need disability insurance and medical for the family. I did research on two reputable companies and had agents write two disability policies up to eighty percent of my income. I also had Tracy write a smaller policy on me with the company we did business with.

I had no idea how I would exit my day job or if I even had the gall to leave at all. After considering how long I had been with the company and all of the benefits, things began to get a little scary. As I continued to perform my daily duties, I began to notice my left leg was gradually becoming weak. Off and on for several weeks I barely had enough strength to engage the clutch. After experiencing this type of discomfort for a week or so the discomfort seemed to have gone away, only to reappear at a later date. I was able to endure these complications for a few months, and then other things began to take place.

I experienced extreme flickering of the eye lids, much too often. Blurred vision and dizziness were added to the list of complications, to say the least. When I began to experience numbness and electric shocks in my stomach and testes, the Katt then knew something was terribly wrong. I wondered how long I could rely on my expertise as a truck driver. It was in the blazing summer heat without air conditioning, while driving the freeways; I recall my eyes getting so full of water I could not see.

The California smog was horrendous and I relied on my instinct and experience to prevent me from crashing into other vehicles. I distinctly remember closing one eye, blotting the other one with my hand, and slowing down as I listened to the sound of the freeway for visibility. Many times, when having these little episodes, I would exit the freeway as soon as possible and take the streets back to the terminal.

After kicking my barrels off, I sat in the driver's room with my head down. I knew I couldn't continue since my condition was progressively getting worse. I have often heard it said that a cat has 9 lives, but I knew I might be pushing this thing just a little too far, therefore, I said to myself, "Wait just a minute Kattman, you have said many, many times that you wanted to leave this place and walk away smelling like a rose, and never look back, so disability might be just the way to go, I thought.

Once again, I began pulling my own chain. In-fact, I savored the moment, "You have medical and dental insurance with the company. You are fully vested with more than twenty years of service, and besides that, you have long-term disability. I applauded myself for having three non-company related disability policies. Man, you can't beat that with an egg beater. You better get out of here while you can still smell the roses." I couldn't fathom the thought of dying and some other dude being with my Tracy.

I needed to be conscientious and get a grip on my health issues, otherwise, I might not be around to smell anything, therefore I wisely sought medical advice. I was referred to a doctor near the job who began costly examinations. I obtained an excuse not to report for work during that period of testing. I guarantee you; I wore every type of medical apparatus from heart monitors to dog collars. After all of those tests and exams, doctor Feel Good still couldn't find anything medically wrong.

He sat me down and questioned my life style, wanting to know whether or not I had any other contact outside of the marriage. I assured him that this was not the case. He qualified his question by saying, "Mister Katt, I have to ask that question in order to eliminate any other possibilities." I told him that the answer was still "no." He dared not to ask the next obvious question. The good doctor had exhausted all conceivable tests possible and everything had come up negative. He was leaning toward sexually transmitted diseases, but the blood test in no way confirmed his suspicion.

He really seemed to be baffled. Then he said to me, "There is one other thing we can do."

"What is that?" I asked.

He said, "We can do a MRI, and I must tell you the MRI is quite expensive, but it will tell us if anything suspicious is going on with your brain." At that time MRI's were not very common. It was available in some of the hospitals and only in a few selective areas. The doctor had a MRI machine in a trailer at the back of his property where other doctors sent their patients for this unique service.

I was very happy that this invention was available during my era of illness. There was a computer linked to the MRI scanner that created an image of the area being scanned and subsequently displayed it on a monitor.

When most physicians learn about a new technology, they usually cross their legs and spend more time talking about it than they do discussing your medical problem, as if this makes them more intellectual. After the MRI films came back we talked about his findings. He says, "I am not a neurologist, but it looks like you may have Multiple Sclerosis (MS). The X-ray shows that you have lesions on the brain, also known as plaque. You need to see a specialist. If you don't know of one, I can refer you to someone in this area." I told him I would like to find a neurologist in the area where I lived. We parted company as I took the X-rays with me; after all, I paid big bucks for that little procedure.

Since Tracy worked for a law firm, there was no better place to inquire about a good certified neurologist. Sure enough, one of the partners father had MS and was being treated by a neurologist that was board certified in the next town. The attorney made a call to Dr. Malcolm L. Wright and his office called me and set up an appointment for me to see him.

I took my Magnetic Resonance Imaging (MRI) films with me. Dr. Wright confirmed Dr. Feel Good's suspicion of MS. Dr. Wright was more exact than any. After viewing the X-rays, he began checking my vision and coordination. He used sharp objects to check for paralysis. He had me walk from one side of the room and back as he watched my gait. He said to me, "Sit on the exam table and lift both arms and don't let me pull them down. Oh yes, you have MS, I will have to do a spinal tap to see if the bands in your spinal fluid verify my finding."

He turned to the x-rays and informed me that multiple sclerosis is characterized by a gradual destruction of myelin, the white matter of the brain and spinal cord. Many small white specks called plaque appear scattered throughout the myelin and interfere with the normal function of nerve pathways. The MRI showed that I had three lesions on the right side of the brain and a smaller one on the left.

"I want you to know, "he says, "The symptoms of MS vary, depending on the affected areas of the brain and spinal cord. You have experienced some of the symptoms, but not all of them. This is a degenerative disorder which symptoms include a staggering gait, blurred vision, dizziness, numbness, breathing difficulty, weakness of the arms and legs, tremors, slurred speech, bladder and bowel problems and sometimes emotional problems." He goes on to add, "Stay out of the sun because that will exacerbate your condition."

Doctor Wright helped me to avoid erroneous thinking. Perhaps this disease is just a punk, but it is potentially lethal. He asked, "What type of work do you do? My answer was, "truck driver," He said "You can't do that anymore."

"Do you have insurance other than State Disability and medical?

"I do."

"I suppose you have Long Term Disability?

"I do."

"Okay that's good," he says. "When your State Disability runs out and Long Term kicks in, you will have to file for Social Security, but don't worry about the paperwork because we will take care of that for you." He gave me a wink. "Meanwhile, go out front and get scheduled for a spinal tap." I liked Dr. Wright immediately. He was kind of young, but very intelligent, friendly, sort of hip-like and sure of himself.

While waiting for my next appointment, suddenly I was hit with severe back pains and started passing blood in the urine. Since this was something new, Tracy called Dr. Wright and he advised her to bring me in right away. After examining me, he sent me to the hospital for a series of x-rays. It turned out that I had a kidney stone that was trying to pass. Unfortunately, this was just another problem to add to my long list of complications I have to admit, the attending technicians at the hospital were super nice. One of them said to me, "So, Dr. Wright is your doctor." "He sure is," I said. "Do you know him?" "Yes I do." she said. My next question was, "Is he good?" She responded by saying, "Oh yes, he's cocky, but he's good." I gave a big smile because that was right up my alley.

Six months had now passed and I got a letter from Long Term Disability advising me that I would be receiving LTD benefits for as long as I am totally disabled, therefore, I must file for Social

Security benefit. The letter also stated that if I did not apply, my LTD benefits would be discontinued

Without hesitation, the very next day, I immediately called for an appointment at the local Social Security office. I was mailed an application and instructed to return it the day of my appointment. I am now about to experience injustices of the social kind. The following two pages are pictures of some Social Security buildings located throughout Los Angeles and Los Angeles County.

Los Angeles County Social Security Offices
taken by Paula Hines

Over two thousand people go through doors like these each day for one reason or another. The population of Los Angeles and Los Angeles County well exceeds nine million people. Of all persons 21 to 64 years of age, over 500,000 of them are disabled and unemployed. In the disabled arena, females are the leaders. Sad to say though, many of them will die before they or their dependants are recipients of any Social Security benefits.

My appointment day arrived and I was there ahead of time to sign in. As usual, with an establishment like this, they never get you in on time. After waiting for forty- six minutes my name was called. Without an apology for the wait, I was asked if I brought my application with me. We then went through the verification phase. "Mister Katt, do you have a middle name? "Yes, I do, it's Rea." "Is that spelled, R-A-Y?" "No," I responded, "it's R-E-A."

Those type of questions lasted for another five minutes. To beat all, she then went back to verify my social security number once again. My immediate response was "Kat Double-O-Soul," when transposed reads 528-00-7085. She finally keyed all pertinent information into the computer.

"Mister Katt," she says, "I have good news for you."

"What's that?" I asked.

"You have lots of money up there." She also informed me that I didn't need an attorney at this time.

That was lie number One. I had no experience in filing for Social Security; therefore I probably would have been better off with three attorneys. She also told me in confidence that my illness does not have to be visible in order to receive Social Security benefits. That was lie number Two. Let me ask you something, just go back to chapter three and take another good look at my picture and tell me if you think a young black man that looked as good as I did, could just waltz into a Social Security office and they give him benefits? I don't think so. I tell you, this is where my experience of social injustices began.

After that tiring interview and being told I would hear from the Administration in sixty days she bid me good luck. I was ready for home. Whether this thing was psychological or not, I could feel my strength slowly diminishing, being listless as never before I crawled into bed, which proved to be my best option at the time.

Approximately sixty days had passed when I received a letter from the State of California –Health and Welfare Agency, stating:

"Your claim for disability benefits under the Social Security Act has been reviewed and more information is needed about your Multiple Sclerosis, stress, and poor vision. It is necessary that you be examined at no cost to you by:

Lawrence P. Kooche M.D., Inc
3310 Pewee Circle.
Los Angeles County 90001
Nerve-Mental Exam

I go into Dr. Kooche's office. They had me sitting in a little room with only a chair and table and a child's puzzle taken apart laying there in wait. I sat isolated, staring at that silly thing for seven minutes. His assistant bursts in, "Mr. Katt, can you put that puzzle together?"

"I suppose so." My first instinct was to take both hands and push the puzzle together into one pile and leave it, nevertheless, before I could finish putting it together she was back saying, "That's good."

"Please step next door and Dr. K will see you," so I was told.

Dr. Kooche was in his late fifties, had a full head of white hair, white goatee, and white beard. He had a likely resemblance to a white Billy goat. He wanted to know if I remembered my age and who was the President of the United States? What is the president's wife's name? Why I wore a mustache? I was wondering why his mama wore a mustache.

I suppose it was his game plan, or out of curiosity he asked me that last question. Of course, this was only the beginning of his stupid questions. What's your wife name? How long have you been married? How often do you and your wife bump the monkey? In other words, how often did my wife and I have sexual relations? If I had known what I know now, I would have asked him how often his granny bumped the monkey.

He wanted to know my religious affiliation. That was one question I wished I had never answered and didn't realize that the question was off limits. In my opinion, Lawrence Paul Kooche was a quack. In the professional community he is referred to as a half-ass, one half medical Doctor, the other half he claims to be a Psychiatrist. Regardless of his claim, in my opinion, he's as worthless as tits on a bull. Dr. Kooche is the very beginning of the claimant's worst nightmare. Most of his questions were precisely designed for an ambush of which the Administrative Law Judge used to his benefit sometime later.

Several months had passed by and I received a denial letter.

Social Security Notice
Department of Health and Human Services
Social Security Administration
Date --/--/----
SS# 528-00-7085

Melvin Rea Katt
4444 Boogie Woogie Ave.
Los Angeles County 90009

We have determined that you are not entitled for disability benefits based on the claim you filed. However, you may appeal this determination if you still think you are disabled.

We have determined that your condition does not keep you from working. We considered the medical and other information, your age, education, training, and work experience in determining how your condition affects your ability to work.

The following reports were used in deciding your claim:

Malcolm L Wright, M.D.
Harry C. Feel Good, M.D.
Lawrence P. Kooche, M.D. Inc

You said you are unable to work because of multiple sclerosis, dizziness, blurred vision, numbness in hands and right leg, headaches, stress and the lack of balance. The medical evidence shows that you do have multiple sclerosis (early stage) but you do not show conditions which would cause significant limitation in carrying out your normal activities.

You should never engage in balancing or climbing, avoid heights, moving machinery and open flames. The evidence shows that you have satisfactory vision and are able to use and move your right leg in an appropriate manner. You are limited in handling objects with your right hand due to decreased grip strength. Although you may feel stressed at times, the medical evidence shows that you are able to think, act and communicate in your best interests. We realize that your condition keeps you from doing your previous job as a truck driver but it does not prevent you from doing lighter work.

If your condition gets worse and keeps you from working, write, call, or visit any Social Security office about filing another application. The determination on your claim was made by an agency of the State. It was not made by your doctor or by other people or agencies writing reports about you. However, any evidence they give us was used in making this determination. Doctors and other people in the State agency who are trained in disability evaluation reviewed the evidence and made the determination based on Social Security laws and regulations.

In addition, you are not entitled to any other benefits based on this application. If you apply for other benefits, you will receive a separate notice when a decision is made on that claim(s).

Your Right To Appeal

If you think we are wrong, you can ask that the determination be looked at by a different person. This is called reconsideration. If you want reconsideration, you must ask for it within 60 days from the date you receive this notice. Your request must be made in writing through any Social Security office. Be sure to tell us your name, Social Security number and why you think we are wrong.

Regional Commissioner

All of you who now think that the Department of Health and Human serves are perfectly honest, don't be so kind. Logistically speaking their letter was no more than self-serving. I read an article released in the mid 1900's entitled 69% rejected. The source of this material is the Social Security Administration. The Social Security Administration rejects 691 disability claims out of every 1,000 it receives. That means approximately 7 out of every 10 people who apply never collect Social Security benefits for their claim.

Of the 309 who collect, a good number do so only after waiting many months for their claims to go through a lengthy four-step appeals process. If your claim is rejected in the first step, you then have less than a 9 percent chance of ever collecting. Are the claimants who are rejected by the Administration really capable of working? The records show many apparently aren't capable of holding a job.

I am now entering the second step of the appeals process. I employed the services of Attorney Cotton Foot T. Simmons of Chatsworth, California to assist me with the request for reconsideration. I must tell you, asking the Administration for reconsideration is definitely the easy part. Willingness on the Administration's part to change their decision is where things get a little funky. My second letter of disapproval demonstrates the Administration's ability to vacillate. After reading their second denial letter I knew that I had been thrown into the nine percentile. Perhaps you should take a close look at this second letter.

Department of Health and Human Services
Social Security Administration
Baltimore, Maryland 21235

Melvin Rea Katt
4444 Boogie Woogie Ave
Los Angeles County 90009

Upon receipt of your request for reconsideration, we had your claim independently reviewed by a physician and disability examiner in the State agency which works with us in making disability determinations. The evidence in your case has been thoroughly evaluated, this includes the medical evidence and the additional information received since the original decision. We find that the previous determination denying your claim was proper under the law.

The following reports were considered in deciding your claim:

- Dr. L. P. Kooche, East Valley Hospital
- Dr. M. L Wright

You said that you are unable to work because of multiple sclerosis and depression. After another review of your file, the medical evidence shows that you are able to move your arms, legs and back in a satisfactory manner. There is no significant evidence of lost of control due to muscle weakness or nerve damage. The evidence in the file shows no significant damage to your eyesight, heart, kidneys, lungs or liver. The evidence shows that you are able to think, remember, and follow basic instructions and act in your own interest. Based on the evidence in the file your condition does not limit your ability to perform work related activities and you should be able to perform the duties of truck driver.

If you believe that this reconsideration determination is not correct, you may request a hearing before an Administrative Law Judge. If you want a hearing, you must request it no later than 60 days from the date you receive this notice.

Regional Commissioner

Since the Administration professed to be such an expert in the law I thought for sure they would have known it was in violation of the Department of Transportation (D.O.T) Regulations for me to operate a commercial vehicle in my present condition. Those guys telling me in writing I could perform the duties of a truck driver infuriated the good doctor. He drafted a blistering letter to the Administration in this form:

Department of Health and Human Services
Social Security Administration
Baltimore, Maryland 21235

Attn: Regional Commissioner

Dear Sir:

RE:Melvin Rea Katt
SS# 528-00-7085

I am in receipt of your communiqué from the Social Security office to Melvin Rea Katt that states that he should be able to perform his duties as a truck driver based on the fact that he has no examination changes.

While I am in agreement that his examination does not show any change grossly, he does have some recent decrement in vision, visual acuity dropping to 20/50 on the right and 20/100 on the left, which may signal some worsening of his demyelinating disease; please be advised that he does have demyelinating disease and it is radio graphically proven on the basis of his MRI scan.

The problem arises from the fact that people in your level of responsibility aren't able to understand that this gentleman has a potentially lethal disease, if he were to go back to work; the neurological exam could potentially change because of multiple factors that would be brought to bear on his disease by returning to work. If this were the case and he were to have a worsening of his neurological function, i.e., loss of use of his legs, change in control of bowel and bladder, sensory change, imbalance, visual acuity changes still further yet, or anything else that might be precipitated by return to work that you feel is justifiable in his case, he would lose these functions and never regain them. The risk of loss of his functions is not worth the risk of trying to put him back to work. I am sure you would not want to be responsible for having a patient go back to work and then have them lose the use of their legs from the stress induced by returning to the job. I know that you would not want to have to go to bed every night aware of the fact that your decision had changed a person's life and had caused irretrievable neurological damage that could never be regained.

Please be advised that these kinds of decisions are important. I realize you don't see this man every day the way I do as his private physician, and you aren't sensitive and understanding of his position and his responsibilities in life, and the disaster that would be precipitated by further loss of neurological function.

I am also advised that the types of consultants you have usually are not qualified individuals and I would like to have substantiation to the fact that his case was reviewed by a Board Certified Neurologist and especially one that is qualified in the area, by special training, to be an authority on multiple scleroses.

When you can substantiate that this type of individual has reviewed this case, and in fact even has examined this patient, and he indeed states that the patient is able to go back to work, then and only then would I allow the patient to subject himself to the risk of returning to work. I refuse to take the responsibility, nor do I feel comfortable in allowing you to take the responsibility of having a man return to work and lose function of his legs, bowel and bladder, sensory function of the body, his eyes, or even speech or swallowing function, things that could never, ever be regained once they are lost in this disease.

If you have any comments or thoughts that you wish to communicate with me regarding Mr. Katt's case, please be advised that I am ready, willing and able to discuss them with you at your convenience.

Sincerely,

Malcolm P. Wright, M.D., F. A. A.P.

CHAPTER EIGHT

ALL OF YOU MATURE persons will have to admit that it took some balls to compose a letter like that. Dr. Wright earnestly felt that I was experiencing social injustice. No other doctor would have gone out on a limb as he did. The Administration received Dr. Wright's letter as well as my request for a hearing before an Administrative Law Judge.

I have you to know, that I was assigned the worst judge in the nation, the notorious Administrative Law Judge H.P. Muthah, and he's a real mutha-fuh-yah. He was probably in his mid-seventies and evil as a rattle snake. He was bald as an eagle with the exception of a few sprigs here and there. Really, he reminded me of a buzzard (albino) because of what I remembered about a buzzard, once he messes on you, you can't ever get it off. Judge Muthah was described as: the damnedest, the rudest, the meanest, and the most vindictive judge you could ever meet.

The scene was about to move to the Federal X building in San Bernardino, California. Sixty days before the hearing Judge Muthah came after me with a subpoena for copies of our IRS Form 1040, with all attachments and schedules for the year commencing with the year after disability began.

This was an effort to sabotage my claim. My counselor knew that submitting to the judge's request would not be in my best interest, therefore counsel on my behalf sanitized portions of the 1040 forms stating, "that counsel on behalf of claimant Melvin Rea Katt hereby move to quash the subpoena to my client for copies of IRS Form 1040 with all attachment and schedules for year in question on the ground that Federal Income Tax Returns

115

are privileged from disclosure pursuant to Internal Revenue Code, Title 26."

While there are certain exceptions to the blanket privilege provided in 26 U.S.C. Section 6103, the only exceptions for Social Security purposes are set at 26 U.S.C. Section 6103(1), (1) and refer to disclosure of FICA tax and to certain situations regarding collection of child support. See Tierney v. Schweiker, 718 F. 2d (9th cir. 1983).

Despite the invalidity of the subpoena, we are providing some information, without waiving any privilege, in the interest of moving this claim forward as rapidly as possible.

The information attached covers all wages attributed Mr. and Mrs. Katt for the year in question. Their other income, if any, is not properly discoverable.

The moment the hearing began it became obvious that Judge Muthah had an erection for both me and my attorney. He began hammering away at what he called being engaged in substantial gainful activity during the disability phase. One of his questions was; Who drove me to the hearing? He asked to see my driver's license. He used Lawrence Kooche's inquiry, inferring that I was associating with a few religious friends occasionally amounted to proselytizing.

He asks me to describe my quality of performance as a truck driver. I admitted that I was very good and burst into tears. I did not understand the real cause for the downpour but, it didn't faze Judge Muthah not one little bit. He turned his attention to the vocational expert and asked if my skills could be transferred. He said they could. Attorney Cotton Foot Simmons asked for the locations. He gave an uneducated reply like, Bakersfield, and Indio, California. Surely he should have known that those areas were the hottest in the Northern and Southern part of California.

I was totally wiped out after the hearing. He hung me out to dry. I felt like I had been in a hatchet fight and everyone had a hatchet except me. I was beat up pretty badly. In my opinion at the time, Judge Muthah was a professional killer, operating a rancid business. I remained in bed for two weeks without any activity. Mental anguish, edgy and lack of strength to hold on to my coffee cup was just some of the problems I was experiencing at the time.

I once thought that Social Security was like a mother. If the time were to come when I was down and out, Social Security would take me in its blanket and secure me like a mother. I was totally mystified. It was my opinion at the time that Social Security was much like a prostitution ring; the disabled are violated by the practitioners and consequently paid a fee for doing such a good job.

Before long I was gradually getting a little of my strength back and anger began to dissipate somewhat, but at the time I was taking numerous medications and all medicines have side effects. I have now become a fat cat and disturbing the peace. I was snoring something furious. Amitriptylene (Elavil) was the culprit, I had gained weight to the point I could no longer bottom my shirt collar. My general practitioner did nothing to change the medicine but asked a couple of questions instead, "How many meals do you eat a day? What time do you eat supper? Then he goes, "Six o'clock is late enough to eat. You don't need no energy to sleep." I have him to know, Black folks eat whenever it's available.

When I first started taking medicine for MS, it came in every color in the rainbow, some I was taking in the morning, through the day, others at night, some with food and some without food and believe it or not, I had to make notes to keep everything straight.

As expected, we received correspondence from the Administration advising us of their decision to deny benefits. In his decision Judge Muthah suggested that I had a lack of motivation to return to work because of receiving disability income.

At that particular time we weren't doing too badly financially. I was receiving LTD and two of the private policies were kicking.

In the interim, we laid the ground work for a retrial by writing to the Social Security Administration Appeals Council advising that counsel raised the issues of Judge Muthah's bias, and the Administration, I am sure, is interested not only in claimant's receiving an unbiased hearing, but that the actual hearing appears to be fair. Therefore, a remand to a judge other than Judge Muthah is proper and necessary.

Exhibit "A" was submitted: Request for Review of Hearing Decision Order and Hearing Tapes.

The administrative law judge based his decision on a credibility determination which is permeated with H.P. Muthah's bias. In this connection attention is specifically invited to the third full paragraph of page 7 of the decision.

Not only did Judge Muthah engage in prohibited squat and squirm adjudication Perminter v. Heckler, 765 F. 2d 870, 872 (9th cir. 1985) but he turned the entire claim into a credibility determination found the claimant to be not credible and thereupon found the claimant to be not disabled, a practice specifically prohibited in Jones v. Heckler, 760 F. 2d 993 (9th cir. 1985).

Judge Muthah's bias is further demonstrated by issuing a subpoena to claimant for his income Tax Records, see Exhibit 29.

What has been set out above is more than required to obtain a remand to a judge other than H.P. Muthah. If this is not to happen claimant requests a copy of the hearing tape. After its receipt counsel will provide further and detailed argument.

A lot of work went into the argument for an appeal. I was impressed the argument set aside for the review. Take a look.

Supplemental Argument to Request for Review

The Administrative Law Judge's decision is improper in several particulars and at the very least requires a remand. However in view of the quality of the decision, any remand should be to an Administrative Law Judge other than Administrative Law Judge Muthah.

The decision raises the following major issues: (1) no fair hearing. Counsel does not raise any objection to the conduct of the hearing itself, but to the content of the decision which raises serious questions of propriety. (2) The finding in the decision that Mr. Katt performed substantial gainful activity through the year in question not only lacked substantial evidence in the record but the treatment of the area demonstrates bias. (3) The consideration of the medical evidence.

The decision (with regard to the period after the questionable date and the claimant was last insured through the same period. (Exhibit 7, page 1) rests on a residual functional assessment by Judge Muthah which was unsupported in the evidence and arrived at by employing improper standards. This area will be considered first. The format of the decision makes difficult to analyze the finding, i.e., there is no mention of inability to perform past relevant work, although this is implied.

Finding 4 reads: The claimant is under a severe impairment as more fully described in the body of the decision which does not meet or equal the listings Lewin v. Schweiker, 654 F. 2d 631 (9ᵗʰ cir. 1981) holds that the Administrative Law Judge's findings should be as comprehensive and analytical as feasible, with subordinate factual foundation on which ultimate factual conclusions are based.

Finding 4, insofar as it deals with equaling listings, not only violates Lewin, but Marcia v. Sullivan, 900 F. 2d 172 (9ᵗʰ cir. 1990) which requires sufficient findings to demonstrate a serious consideration of equaling which may be based on a combination of impairments, or on an alternative test, finding of comparable severity.

A search through the text of the decision reveals a residual functional capacity found by the Administrative Law Judge (additional to that of finding 4) to wit: the implied finding of light and sedentary in finding 5.

The residual functional capacity can be dragged out of page 7, of the decision, first full paragraph light and sedentary and the claimant should not engage in prolonged walking or the frequent use of stairs, should not work at heights or around dangerous unguarded moving machinery, should not work on rough or uneven surfaces, should not be required consistently to perform fine or close visual work, and should not be exposed to temperature extremes (second paragraph, decision, page 7).

The residual functional capacity is not only improper in form but lacks support in the record. The proscription against prolonged walking by itself rules out light work as a starting as light work which requires ability to stand six out of eight hours, SSR 83-10. Surely the Administrative Law Judge did not by not mentioning standing intend to make a distinction between walking and standing. There is no medical evidence supporting such a distinction.

In determining residual functional capacity, if what Judge Muthah did, the Administrative Law Judge exercised on expertise he does not possess and which he cannot obtain by consulting texts.

Day vs. Weinberger 522 f. 2d 1154 (9th cir. 1975) is absolute authority on that point. Moreover, the decision falls afoul of Diaz v. Bowen 644 F. supp. (S.D.N.Y. 1987) which holds the Appeals Counsel cannot draw its own conclusions as to residual functional capacity on the basis of its reading of the medical records.

The members of the Appeals Counsel, who are not physicians, are not qualified to evaluate the correlations between clinical findings and a claimant's functional capacity, Wilson v. Heckler 743 F. 2d 218, 221 (4th cir. 1984).

Judge Muthah who is a minimalist on findings rejected the disability opinion of the treating physician and making it the subject of a specific finding. The impression is disability of Dr. Wright is unpersuasive for the reasons set forth in the decision (finding 6, decision, page 11). As no particular decisional page is referred to the Appeals Counsel, this counsel, and if necessary, the United States District Court must search his lengthy but inadequate decision.

Counsel observes the principal treatment of treating Dr. Wright's records appears to start at the last full paragraph on page 4 and continues through to the last paragraph on page 5. The rules for rejecting the opinions of the treating physician are clear and well established in this Circuit, Magallanes v. Bowen, 881 F 2d 747 (9th cir. 1989) holds that to reject an uncontroversial opinion of claimant's physician, the Administrative Law Judge must present clear and convincing reason for doing so.

To reject an opinion of a treating physician which is conflicted by that of an examining physician, the Administrative Law Judge must make findings setting forth specific, legitimate reasons for doing that are based on substantial evidence in the record. Rodriquez v. Bowen, 876 F. 2d 759 (9th cir. 1989) notes the medical opinion of a claimant's treating physician is entitled to special weight, Embrey v. Bowen, 849 F 2d. 418, 421 (9th cir. 1988) Valencia v. Heckler, 951 F. 2d 1081, 1088 (9th cir. 1985),

The treating physician's opinion is given that deference because he is employed to cure and has a greater opportunity to know and observe the patient as an individual, Sprague v. Secretary, 812 F. 2d 1226 (9th cir. 1987) (citation omitted). However, the treating physician's opinion on the ultimate issue of disability is not necessarily conclusive.

The Administrative Law Judge may disregard the treating physician's opinion, but only by setting forth specific, legitimate reasons for doing so, and this decision must itself be based on substantial evidence. (Cotton v. Bowen, 799 F. 2d 1403, (9th cir. 1986). This burden can be met by providing a detailed summary of the facts and conflicting clinical evidence, along with a reasoned interpretation thereof. Id. Furthermore, the Administrative Law Judge's reasons for rejecting the doctor's opinion must be clear and convincing, Montijo v. secretary, 729 F.2d 599 (9th cir. 1984) at 601; Rhodes v. Schweiker, 729 F. 2d 722, 723 (9th cir. 1981).

According to the summary of Dr. Wright's records provided by the Administrative Law Judge, the clamant first came under the care of Dr, Wright one year seven months prior to these dates and the doctor listed a diagnostic impression of possible demyelinating disease vs. a number of other possibilities. The doctor continued to follow the claimant at two to three month intervals.

The Administrative Law Judge notes although Dr, Wright according to his records, has never entertained any diagnosis other than probable demyelinating disease or probable multiple sclerosis, he reported rather more positively in connection with the present proceeding, under the date test reviled that claimant did in fact have a demyelinating disease which has been radiographically proven.

Such statement is in conflict with his records and with the brain scans which have already been referred to (decision, page 5). In assessing the meaning of the import of the studies, Judge Muthah stepped well beyond the bounds of what is permissible. Not only did he violate the ninth circuit rule set forth in Day, Supra, but he violated established principles providing for what is and what is not proper medical testimony.

Since the Administrative Law Judge is not a medical professional, the substitution of his or her own opinion for that of an expert presenting competent medical evidence is error.

Wilson v. Heckler, 743 F. 2d 218, 221 (4th cir. 1984) reads, in finding that Dr. Marshall's clinical finding did not support his conclusions as to plaintiff's functional limitations, the Administrative Law Judge erroneously exercised an expertise he did not possess in the field of orthopedic medicine". In accordance Taylor v. Heckler, 742 F. 2d 253, 257 (5th cir. 1984); Van Horn v. Schweiker, 717 F. 2d 871, 874 (3rd. cir. 1983); Mc Brayer v. secretary HEW, 712 F. 2d 795, 799 (2nd cir. 1983);

Goodley v.Harris, 608 F. 2d 234, 236 n. 1 (5ᵗʰ cir. 1979); Fowler v. Califano, 596 F. 2d 600, 603 (3ʳᵈ cir. 1979).

Thus Administrative Law Judge Muthah's opinion on what the findings should have shown to substantiate or confirm the clinical diagnosis of the treating physician is of no evidentiary value. For example Judge Muthah's opinion as to whether the size of a white spot on claimant's brain indicates multiple sclerosis has less than no value. It is impertinent.

The Administrative Law Judge refused to accept the opinion of Dr. Wright, not only because he does not believe that the underlying documentation conclusively proves multiple sclerosis, but because, Dr. Wright conflicted his own report by first stating that the patient probably had demyelinating disease or multiple sclerosis and that later he stated the patient did in fact have demyelinating disease which had been radiographically proven and by Dr. Wright having stated that the patient returned to work activities were dangerous to his health and that he later appears to have changed his mind and in a letter which claimant's counsel presented at the time of the hearing, indicating in effect that the claimant could at least try to engage in sedentary work activity.

The letter has been willingly misinterpreted. Dr. Wright said, "a trial of sedentary work would not be illogical in this case but runs the risk of worsening symptoms". (This is exactly in congruent with what the doctor had said before). Dr, Wright added, "my assessment is that in fairness all concerned, the (patient especially) a work retraining trial and sedentary type of work trial would be reasonable to determine if work stress were to exacerbate the patient's symptoms."

This in no way conflicts with what the doctor said before and it is black letter law that the ability to engage in rehabilitation or a trial period of rehabilitation does not equate to substantial gainful activity.

Here the suggestion was not even an attempt to return to part-time work; it was in the nature of a proposed test. The treating physician never suggested that Mr. Katt had the ability to perform full-time regular, sedentary work at any level, which is the test of Cox v. Califano, 587 F. 2d 988 (9th cir. 1978) which holds that a "A willingness to try to engage in rehabilitative activity and a release by one's doctor to try and engage in such an attempt, is clearly not probative of present ability to engage in such activities. Cox also holds that the concept of residual functional capacity involves the ability to tolerate a "sustained daily work routine" at the level of exertion being considered.

The decision seeks support from the opinion of Neal Long, M. D. (consultant). His report did not controvert Dr. Wright's. Both are qualified neurologists. Dr. Long diagnosed possible multiple sclerosis and probable depression but concluded that the diagnosis however had not been firmly established.

In the decision the Administrative Law Judge wrote, referring to Dr. Long, he suggested the claimant was capable of returning to work activity with the avoidance of excessive fatigue, stress, or working in a hot environment". (Decision, page 6) and stated that he was not aware of any scientific literature indicating that a return to work would in of itself worsen the condition of a patient suffering from even an established diagnosis of multiple sclerosis" Id.

This raises two interesting questions. (1) The meaning of "excessive fatigue" which no part of the hypothetical to the vocational expert. That in itself makes the hypothetical incapable of producing substantial evidence. Embrey, supra, holds that hypothetical questions posed to the vocational expert must set out all limitations and restrictions to the particular claimant commented on, including for example, pain and inability to lift certain weights.

If the vocational expert's hypothetical assumptions are incomplete or lack support in the record, the vocational expert's opinion has no evidentiary value. Of course, pain was never mentioned either and that falls afoul of the whole body of ninth circuit law, the latest case being, Delorme v. Sullivan, 924 F. 2d 841 (ninth Circuit, 1991).

If it is to be maintained that excessive fatigue is not easily subject to be quantified to specific limitations it devolves on the Administrative Law Judge to query the medical consultant as he does not lose his obligation to fully and fairly develop the claim, whether or not claimant is represented, Brown v. Heckler, 713 F. 2d 441 (9th cir. 1983.

Such querying, however, would hardly seem necessary as it is clear that excessive fatigue depends very much on the individual and fatigue is a hallmark of the claimant's multiple sclerosis. Indeed, a review of the medical record to the date of hearing unequivocally supports the diagnosis of multiple sclerosis and confirms the acceptance by every examiner that multiple sclerosis or some other demyelinating disease with similar sequelae affected the claimant. A review of the enclosed footnotes will help understand the claimant's disposition.

One month; loss of weight, one month, five pounds; neck pain; constipation- occasional; headaches; lower back pain, sore throat, left side. History of present illness: Age, race, sex, occupation, symptom, location, nature, radiation, aggravated by, relieved by, and current medication for: cardiac risk factors, family history, over 40 years of age, male, black, patient reports dizziness since two weeks ago, aggravated when he bends over before meals, sometimes he loses balance, relieved by resting, after meals.

Nausea is aggravated before meals relieved by analgesics. No diarrhea, epigastric pain relieved by meals, aggravated during the mornings. Headaches, occasional, bi-temporal to the occipital area. Right shoulder pain since he fell down and hit his jaw, he has difficulty lifting arm Id., page 11. The last examination, the diagnosis was demyelinating disease, Id, page 2. Psychiatric consultant Lawrence P. Kooche, M.D., reported twice, first (Exhibit 16) and again (Exhibit 17).

Diagnosis: Axis III- probable multiple sclerosis, mild, history of; Axis I, adjustment disorder with anxious mood, mild, Axis II – 2, Axis -4, Axis v, GAF current: mid forties GAF past six months: mid forties, prognosis: fair (Exhibit 16, page 4).

On the specified date the diagnosis was unchanged the consultant adding: "this gentleman, married, black male has a fairly uneventful history up to recently, when he began having dizzy spells, jerky movements of his right eye, and numbness with tingling in the right hand, as well as in right leg.

These came on briefly several times a day. Two years ago he stopped driving his truck, since the dizziness seems to make it unsafe for him to continue to drive. He has a neurological work-up and that to show some, "plaque formation". He continued to feel rather anxious and somewhat depressed due to his inability to do things as before.

Since the examination onset, he has had some trouble sleeping and continues to have daily headaches. In the mornings he notes soreness in the feet, and has somewhat less stable balance for a while. As the day goes by, however, that seems to disappear. Nevertheless, he continues to be easily fatigued, especially in his lower extremities.

He does very little around the house, but will be at the religious services twice a week and he does see friends occasionally. He appears mildly anxious and depressed, but this has not worsened within the last six months examination.

His concentration is satisfactory and he is able to complete the few tasks he set about to do. He can manage his own funds (Exhibit 17, page 4). Exhibit 18, the medical records of neurologist Malcolm P. Wright M.D., for the period throughout decision comprised of 24 pages contain major reports and substantiating objective testing notations.

The first report is dated on such The doctor provided an extensive history of the course of the illness to that date (Exhibit 18, page 13) noted patient work up by his private physician, Dr. Feel Good, included MRI scan two weeks before which showed bright white objects in the white matter raising the question of demyelinating disease v. vasculitis which was reason for the referral (Exhibit 18, page13).

Dr. Wright had the impression, of: "possible demyelinating disease v. vasculitis vs. cervical stenosis, the latter doubted given the patient's history and physical findings in concert with the laboratory and radiographic findings. The MRI scan raises the question of demyelination centrally with large lesions periventricularly in the coronam radiate of both hemispheres.

This would explain the patient's subtle right hemi paresis and his paresthesia as well reduced endurance and disequilibrium" (Id., page and 16). On a later date, he wrote the impression: remains provable demyelinating disease with stability of exam more testing and a reevaluation was scheduled for one month later.

During this period he was to remain off work (Id, page 12). Two months later, the report of Dr. Wright reported increased symptomatology, difficulty with sleep increased radiating pain in the right shoulder, right leg "right leg feels tired all the time".
"He appears, on today's exam, to be somewhat depressed, which is reasonable and expected response from problem" (Id, page 9). The neurologist's "Impression: "was, "remains probable multiple sclerosis based on CST protein elevation and plaque formation in MRI with negative sedentary rate" (Exhibit 18, page 9).

The plan was to: "began the patient on Elavil 25 mg. h. s. and re-evaluate him in four to six months or sooner should the need arise (Id.). One month later, the neurological follow up evaluation was for acute abdominal pain of unclear etiology.

The doctor again noted claimant has probable MS based on chemical diagnosis. Mr. Katt was to report to the hospital emergency room where he was to be seen by Dr. George (Id., page 8). Two months later, Dr. Wright stated claimant was hospitalized by Dr. George to evaluate a possible kidney stone (Exhibit 18, page 5).

Three months from that date, the impression remained probable multiple sclerosis (Id, page 3). The first month of the next year, Dr. Wright wrote directly to the department Health and Human Services regarding prophylactic restrictions against work because of multiple dangers to claimant's health and even to his life (Id, page 2). Consultant Steve P. Mole, M.D. found that as of the previous year, that vision was good for most moderate visual tasks (Exhibit 19).

Consultant Neal Long, M.D., on his examination did not believe the diagnosis indicate that it is not only the opinion of Dr. Wright that Mr. Katt is suffering from a condition which seriously impedes his ability to function even in a non-work setting, but it is to varying degree the opinion of the other doctors and in that sense the opinion of Dr. Wright are not controverted.

The rule which governs their consideration is clear and convincing, and clear and convincing reason cannot be supplied from Judge Muthah's own medical expertise or his predilections. Much emphasis here has been put on diagnosis and counsel concedes that the diagnosis of a condition does not equate to finding that condition disabling.

In this case, the diagnosis is singularly important because it makes the subjective complaints congruent with a medically determinable condition so that Judge Muthah's assessment of claimant's own residual functional capacity as exaggerated (decision, page 6) is no more proper than his finding that claimant's subjective complaints can be equated no more than credibly minimal in degree" (Id, page 99).

His ultimate, "I find it necessary to comment on claimant's testimony at the time of the hearing. It appeared to be quite histrionic, exaggerated, and over drawn" (Decision, page 7). As a matter of fact the claimant's complaints were precisely of those to be expected from a victim of a demyelinating disease. See Exhibit A attached, multiple sclerosis, page 410 of "Complete Guide of Symptom, Illness and Surgery", H. Winter Griffin, M.D., The body press, 1989 Edition, Los Angeles, California.

Counsel has already requested that the Appeals Council listen to the record as Mr. Katt who has an excellent earnings record was forthcoming and if anything, understated his impairments. The entire decision is apparently a search for evidence on which to base a denial. Cox, Supra, held that in applying the substantial evidence test the court is "obligated to look at the record as a whole and not merely the evidence tending to support a finding" (page 989, 990).

The Administrative Law Judge finds that the ability to drive one time from Los Angeles County to Los Angeles, a distance of twenty nine miles, which ex cathedra states will require driving through some extremely heavy urban traffic (page 8) as evidence of an ability to perform substantial gainful activity.

He does not mention that this trip was necessitated by a death in the family and there is no indication that the traffic was heavy at the time of day the trip was made. That statement was intended to create an impression, not to get the truth (Decision, page 8), any more than the claimant going to religious meetings, one or two times a month, for thirty minutes or more of that day with his Church, proves an ability to perform substantial gainful activity.

The Administrative Law Judge's reliance on the claimant's license not being restricted when it was almost ready for automatic renewal is a low blow as it improperly takes administrative notice of supposed Department of Motor Vehicle regulation in violation of Banks v. Schweiker, 654 F. 2d 637 (9th cir. 1981).

Here is an administrative law judge who makes assumptions about prevalence of heavy traffic from Los Angeles County to Los Angeles but does not bother to remark that lack of a drivers' license in the Los Angeles area with its manifestly inferior public transportation is an extreme handicap, from inability to pick up children from school to going to the doctor.

No one that counsel knows of volunteer's information that will cause a loss of a license as salubrious as this might be. For that matter, the Administrative Law Judge provided no foundation for the assumption that the claimant was under a duty to report his multiple sclerosis.

The Administrative Law Judge points to the claimant having fair visual acuity. But the claimant testified that the vision comes and goes which is entirely consistent with his condition. Testing at any one particular date would not reveal this. There are other examples of basic unfairness in the decision such as, "the claimant according to his testimony has adopted a rather inactive lifestyle, but such adoption is not mandated by any impairment credible established in the present record and appears to be the claimant's own choice" (Decision, page 8).

This is not the case at all! Multiple Sclerosis and its sequelae do entail a severely restricted lifestyle and references again made to the reports of the treating physician and the attachment, Exhibit A hereto.

Lastly, the Administrative Law Judge found that the claimant had performed substantial gainful activity through the time he declared to be disabled. Mr. Katt explained that monies received during that time were for work performed earlier and that he only made one sale near the middle of that year. Even were this sale to have produced a significant return and thus was gainful, it was not substantial.

After being disabling he did not, as he testified, continue to work. If money came in it was in the form of a return for efforts. There is no evidence to the contrary.

The administrative Law Judge improperly subpoenaed the income tax returns of the claimant and on advice of counsel these were refused as the information requested contained information concerning Mrs. Katt and there was no reason to divulge this information to Administrative Law Judge Muthah. The claimant had every right to refuse such information and that very right does not permit the Administrative Law Judge to make any inferences from refusal.

He may not go through the back door. The only evidence of record is that no work was performed after disability date, and there is no reason to doubt Mr. Katt's testimony on that point. He willingly and voluntarily provided that information. For his honesty he should not be penalized.

The suggestion that claimant could work at a sustained competitive level is not only unsupported by the evidence but is a cruel hoax. Kornock v. Harris, 648 F.2d 525 (9th cir. 1980) provides that the ability to work only a few hours a day (such as a few hours a month trying to convert people to his religion) or to work only on an intermittent basis is not the ability to engage in substantial gainful activity and that slight work of an irregular spasmodic character subject to frequent interruptions because of ailments is not substantial gainful activity (at page 527).

Vidal v. Harris 637 F. 2d 710 (9th cir. 1981) provides that alternate jobs proposed for the applicant must involve realistic job opportunities and what is reasonably possible not only what is conceivable that even though capacity, not employability, is the test, the work must be qualified to apply for the job being considered (at page 713).

Clearly, a person without the ability to perform at a consistent pace can neither obtain, nor if he did obtain, retain any job. These adverse factors were referred to in his testimony by vocational expert Monte and the Appeals Counsel in considering the record is urged should pay particular attention to this testimony.

For while the hypothetical or questions were posed by the Administrative Law Judge could not elicit an answer which could provide substantial evidence, the replies to questions of counsel based on the medical condition of the claimant clearly indicate that there was no substantial, or even insubstantial, gainful activity Mr. Katt could consistently perform.

Of course, remand is possible and it would be difficult to argue that it is not an opinion available to the Secretary, but this claimant has already been rung through a wringer and has been accused of malingering by Administrative Law Judge Muthah because he had the good fortune and foresight to purchase disability insurance and maintain employment with the company which provided a disability policy.

This imputation of wrong doing is on the same level as impugning credibility on the ground that the claimant refused to give up his rights to keep his income tax returns from prying eyes.

While this is a proper claim for remand it is equally a proper claim for benefit payment, Varney v. Secretary, (II) 859 F. 2d 1396 (9th cir. 1988) provides that the court will accept the pain testimony (and this includes testimony of limitation of activity) as true and order immediate benefit payments if: (1) there are no additional issues that must be resolved on remand, (2) the Agency decision does not include sufficient, specific finding to reject excess pain complaints (here we are talking about regular, not excess pain which is even stronger) and (3) it is clear that the Administrative Law Judge would be required to award benefits if the pain testimony were credited at page 1400, and 1401.

This should be considered in concert with Salvador v. Sullivan, 917 F. 2d 13 (9th cir. 1990) which holds an Administrative Law Judge's failure to offer any reasons for disregarding a disability opinion of a treating doctor is legal error, mere references to minor inconsistencies in the opinion are not a sufficient statement of reasons for rejecting the opinion together with Mauonis, Supra, (as it is here) it was appropriate to accept the claimant's complaint to a degree alleged since they were supported by x-ray finding and in addition by doctors' reports and opinions, at page 1014.

Here, there is no lack of objective evidence; it is only that the Administrative Law Judge did not find it to meet his expectations of what the medical evidence should contain.

Respectfully Submitted,

Cotton Foot T. Simmons
Attorney for Claimant

CHAPTER NINE

An after-view

FIRST OF ALL, I was more than pleased the way Cotton Foot stuck it to the notorious Judge Muthah's buzzard butt. I was impressed with all of his arguments in repudiating the Judge's ambitions. It was quite impressive when quoting the D.C. Cir. Decision of 1975 in Phillips v. Weinberger. The court wrote, "It has been held, time and again, that the word substantial, does not modify 'gainful' but rather modifies 'activity'.

Thus the activity in which the claimant must be able to engage must not only be 'gainful' but it must also be 'substantial' [citations]". "In this context, 'gainful' activity refers to activity for remuneration. Or profit (or intended for profit, whether or not a profit is realized) 20 CFR section 404.15342 (b). 'Substantial' activity has been defined by the courts as the ability to perform an activity with reasonable regularity [citation]".

This won us another day to fight but, this in no way was a slam-dunk, but a technical reprieve because we had the distinct task of going before that same old demon, Judge H.P. Muthah, for the second time. Counsel was also an older, but a white headed man. I nick-named him Snow White. (Without his knowledge of course) I feared that those two guys were going to be homogeneous.

Cotton Foot surely thought better of showing his face in Judge Muthah's courtroom again. Plan (B) He prepared his female assistant to represent me instead of him. Cotton Foot was old enough to know the leopard wouldn't change his spots.

Here is what I did know, win, lose or draw, Judge Muthah only had two shots at me and he could no longer adjudicate my case. Even at that I felt like I was standing on a three legged stool, but determined to hold on.

As we were preparing for another bout with Judge Muthah, Murphy's Law was enacted upon me. The two insurance companies who were paying my claims notified me that they would no longer pay because I had an active insurance license. The insurance company, which refused to pay anything, did the investigation and strung me along by saying, "we have one more thing to check and we can rap this thing up." They were searching through my dirty underwear, but the Katz's tail was clean as a whistle.

They checked with my neighbors, asking if they ever saw me doing manual labor. Of course, the neighbor across the street tells them, "Oh no, he has an insurance license". This Company therefore so advised the other companies and refunded all of my premiums. Consequently, I knew better than cash the check. We then initiated law suits against all three companies and settled out of court for multiple lumps sums of one hundred sixty five thousands of those pretty little green ones. This transpired exactly one year and six months after the filing date.

It was just past midyear when we were summoned to appear before the Administrative Law Judge. We did our last dance with the Muthah and he was still none yielding and just as obstinate as he had ever been, although, he showed madam attorney a little more respect than he did Cotton Foot. He began by informing me I was still under oath. He still had no intention of giving up on this thing about religion and attempted to linger on that issue. I immediately responded by saying, "that is a low down dirty trick."

"Religion doesn't have anything to do with my illness." He growled and snapped. "Are you not going to answer my question? You heard what I said." I was inclined to lick my tongue out at him. Of course this was my way of sassing him back. His questions were always directed in a scolding manner. It was obvious I wasn't going to answer his question, therefore, he moved on to the next one, as he had turned red. I was in no way willing to relinquish my rights in an atmosphere of obnoxious fervor and especially for the likes of Judge Muthah.

The vocational expert had his little say. After that, the Judge wanted to know if counsel had any questions for the vocational expert. Counsel declined and asked if claimant had any questions for the vocational expert. I declined, but couldn't pass up this grand opportunity. Since Counsel had given me the nod I supposed responding was in order. So you think MS is just a punk, do you not?" He paused – "I don't understand," he said. I asked counselor to rephrase my question.

"Mr. Monte, do you feel that multiple sclerosis is weak or a non serious disease?" "I am not sure," was his reply. "Do you have other questions Mr. Katt?" "No thanks". I am exactly four and one half years older since I announced my disability. More and more symptoms listed on the previous general information page began to manifest themselves. Thankfully I did not have the deadly symptoms that would wreck a marriage.

Happy to say, at present time I didn't have problems in regard to the conjugal issues, I was still able to swing old Tom. Although MS packed a devastating blow I never became indolent. My mother-in-law teasingly would sometimes ask "How is old Tom?" I smiled and said, "I was lying about old Tom all along." She always laughed and said, "I'm hip." Of course there were other issues that had to be addressed. For an example, what I once thought would be a future thriving cattle business had to be reconsidered because of my illness.

Becoming a big time cattle rancher within the next five years had to be put on hold. If I did any kind of ranching it would have to be strictly therapeutic. My cousin T.C. is now on dialysis and my father-in-law is losing more of my cattle than he leave standing and besides that Pop's was charging me a small fortune to feed them. During the winter months more than fifty percent of the cows ended up being buzzard bait. Of course Tracy wanted to know what we were going to do about that. I frankly told her when I receive my Social Security benefits, we are not leaving, we are gone.

Sixty days after the hearing we received what was expected. It was the second denial notice of its kind. Judge Muthah had such an erection for socialistic fervor his comments were not the twilight of an opinion but, rather the falsification of his finding to authenticate his decision. He said of one disabled mechanic, "He was still working because he had grease under his finger nails.

That could not have been observable because the Judge and claimant are twenty five feet apart and both parties had to make use of the microphones. Nonetheless, there was one good thing about this day Judge Muthah was about to become history. School was out. My encounters with the Administrative Law Judge Muthah were over.

I had a brief celebration with Cotton Foot in his office there in Chatsworth and was told I did a very good job at the hearing. He nodded to me saying, "My boy, when you follow the rule, you get screwed." Having said that he added, "It's now time for all of us to get paid". He informed me that he knew Judge Muthah would not rescind, he would remain the same butt hole he's always been and that was his reason for using his assistant at the second hearing. Knowing that the Administrative Law Judge Muthah was a cold piece of work, he would surely defy justice once again and make it easier to be granted a retrial with another judge.

The second request for an appeal was pretty much the same as the first one. Cotton Foot and I once again went on the offensive as we exploited Judge Muthah's disregard for judicial law while being open and notorious for verbalizing his bias opinions. Although the Administrative Law Judge was very much aware of our legal argument but, due to his obstinacy it was apparent he would in no way change his opinion and that is why we felt that the Administration would surely grant us a new hearing before another Judge.

In due process we had to always remember the Social Security Administration was not our friend. Just one slip up and we would have to start all over again. In any and all cases where the claimant does not appear to have one foot in the grave and the other one on a banana peel, he needs an attorney who comes dressed to fight. The Administration often denies appeals on the basis of non-compliance. They claimed the Administration did not receive the request within the allotted time frame. To circumvent this little trick we always sent our correspondences certified. Quiet as keep the Appeals Council has eyes, but, they cannot see. They have knowledge, but, will not discern.

Nonetheless, you will most likely witness a response as I did: The Appeals Council has concluded that there is no basis under the above regulation for granting your request for review. Accordingly, your request is denied and the Administrative Law Judge's decision stands as a final decision of the Secretary in your case. In reaching this conclusion, the Appeals Council carefully considered each of the contentions raised by your attorney in his letter of this date, but decided that these contentions do not provide a basis for changing the Administrative Law Judge's decision.

Your attorney contends that you did not receive a fair, unbiased hearing. The Appeals Council does not agree. The council's audit of the hearing and its comprehensive review of the evidence of record reveal that the Administrative Law Judge concluded an impartial hearing, and that he reached a decision that is consistent with the record in its entirety. The Council is unable to find any indication of impropriety on the part of the Administrative Law Judge in conducting the hearing or in his consideration of the evidence.

In addition to the above, the Council does not find any evidence, either objective or subjective, showing that you have been precluded from performing non-strenuous light and sedentary work for any continuous 12 month period commencing on or after your alleged onset of disability, and in particular the jobs cited by the vocational expert who took all of your functional limitations into account, as well as your age, education and work experience. In summary, the council is of the opinion that the Administrative Law Judge's decision is supported by substantial evidence.

If you desire a court review of the Administrative Law Judge's decision, you may commence a civil action by filing a complaint in the United States District Court for the judicial district in which you reside within sixty (60) days from the date receipt of this letter. It will be presumed that this letter is received within five (5) days after the date shown above unless a reasonable showing to the contrary is made.

The complaint should name the Secretary of Health and Human Services as the defendant and should include the Social Security numbers (s) shown at the top of this notice. The right to court review is provided for in section 205 (g) of the Social Security Act, as amended (42 U.S.C. 405 (g) for claims under Title II and in Section 1631 (3) of the Act (42 U.S.C. 1383 (c) (3) for claims under Title XVI.

If a civil action is commenced, the Secretary must be served by sending a copy of the summons and complaint by registered or certified mail to the general counsel of the Department of Health and Human Services at Washington, D.C. 20201. In addition, you must serve the United States Attorney for the district in which you file your complaint and the Attorney general of the United States, as provided in the Federal Rules of Civil Procedure. Administrative Appeals Judge.

Just prior to my fourth year bout with the Social Security Administration I requested my medical doctor to refer me to a Psychiatrist. Surely this would help me at my next weigh in. In fact, my visits to Dr. Zing and his findings became a part of the records. Now we had more tools to use. During the appeals process, we filed a second Title II application after Judge Muthah's second denial.

This claim was denied at the initial and reconsideration levels, and we filed a request for hearing thereafter. Good cause was found for a late filing of the request for hearing. A hearing on both Title II applications was held in Orange, California late that year. I appeared and testified at the hearing, I was represented by Cotton Foot T. Simmons. Also present was a medical expert and specialist in internal medicine who was obliged to testify.

The issues in both Title II applications were whether I was under a disability as defined by the Social Security Act and, if so, when the disability commenced, the duration of the disability, and whether the insured status requirements of the Act are met for the purpose of entitlement to a period of disability and disability insurance benefits. All evidence had to be evaluated.

The specific development ordered by the Appeals Council was carefully followed. The issues presented by both Title II applications were the same and involved the same part and facts, therefore, the decision must be applicable to both applications. In other words, the Administrative Law Judge Muthah messed up.

After a thorough evaluation of the record and my testimony, it was concluded that I had been disabled since the outset of my claim and met the insured status requirements of the Social Security Act on that day and thereafter. It was also found that I had not engaged in any substantial gainful activity regarding my earnings subsequent to my alleged disability onset date; however, evidence submitted in conjunction with the current hearing showed that the earnings were primarily my wife Tracy's and my contribution to the business did not amount to substantial gainful activity.

This administrative law judge (ALJ) did find that I indeed had multiple sclerosis, which is considered to be "severe" under the Social Security regulation. The medical reports from my treating physician, Dr. Malcolm P. Wright M.D., a neurologist, clearly documented this diagnosis, supported objective testing and clinical findings. His most recent dated report provided a detailed summary of my signs and symptoms, including my severe fatigue which is directly caused by the multiple sclerosis.

Because of the extensive medical evidence in the record and in order to clarify the nature and severity of my impairments, the testimony of the expert, Dr. Solomon Isaac, was taken. Dr. Isaac testified that I equaled the requirements of section 11.09C of my diagnosis of the listings, citing my diagnosis of multiple sclerosis confirmed by MRI scans, blurred vision, and weakness of the right side of the body, a slow and difficult gait, depression, and memory lapse.

Therefore, based on a thorough analysis of all the evidence, including the testimony of the medical expert, the ALJ found that my multiple sclerosis equals the requirements of section 11.09C of Appendix 1 to Subpart P of Regulations No. 4. Therefore, it was the decision of the ALJ that I had been under a "disability" as defined in the Social Security Act commencing from the outset and continuing through the date of his decision. (1)The finding was totally invigorating, knowing that the ALJ found me not to have engaged in substantial gainful activity since filing the claim.

Of course that meant all back pay which amounted to more than sixty thousand dollars. (2) The decision was good for my case but not for my well being. The ALJ found that my impairment was considered to be "Severe" under the Social Security Act which is multiple sclerosis. (3) The severity of my impairment equals the requirements of section 11.09C, Appendix 1, Subpart P, Regulation No. 4 since the onset. (4) I had been under a disability since onset filing. (5) Decision: based on the Title II application filed, I was entitled to a period of disability beginning five years prior to this date when disability was filed and to disability insurance benefits under section 216 (i) and 223, respectively, of the Social Security Act, and the disability has continued through at least the date of this decision.

First of all, The Katt felt marvelous that day. After I left the hearing I knew we had won with both hands down. Thanks to the Administrative Law Judge H.P. Muthah. If he hadn't been such a jack-ass, I probably wouldn't have ever won. After thinking more serious about this matter, I realized, the win was bitter sweet. Basically, I threw away all my professional licenses I worked hard to attain and had been proud of. This was primarily the results of Judge Muthah's pissing, moaning and groaning. To a person looking on for the first time, it would appear that I would receive a whole lot of money from Social Security. But, hold on. Not so fast. I did, but it wasn't for keeps.

There is another side to this story. LTD was paying approximately sixty percent of my salary and the rule of thumb is when Social Security kicks in, the receiver must reimburse LTD, and that is why the disabled person is threatened if he does not file for Social Security in a timely fashion. The record indicated I was indebted to LTD for fifty five thousand dollars; therefore it was time to negotiate.

Understandably I had incurred so much expense over that long period of time I only had fifty two thousand dollars left. At least that's what I told them. I asked if they would please accept the fifty two thousand dollars as payment in full. Not to my surprise LTD called me up a few days later and accepted my offer if I agreed to drop that amount in the mail the next day. I went over to Tracy and said, "Hey baby, guess what? I just saved us three thousand dollars."

It appears I now have everything in the bag. Our oldest son was graduating in May from a five year course at a local university (Cal. Poly Pomona) Our second son was graduating from a local high school in June and was accepted at Texas A&M University. Last but not least, our daughter was moving on to high school. Since California is considered a rat race, and, since all our children had graduated from a difference level of academics, Tracy and I thought it was time to make a move.

The four of us packed our things and moved to Texas where we had already purchased sixteen acres of land parallel to my parent's property and constructed a four bedroom flat. Life is a lot less stressful here in Texas. We have three creek ponds flowing with fresh spring water full of White Perch, Channel Cats, and Big Mouth Bass to catch at my leisure. With the passing of time Tracy and I are able to enjoy the presence of our first grandchild, Ethan Alexander.

Our oldest grandson Ethan Alexander